CW00401402

Other Books by Harriet Steel

Becoming Lola

Salvation

City of Dreams

Following the Dream

Dancing and Other Stories

The Inspector de Silva Mysteries

Trouble in Nuala

Dark Clouds over Nuala

Offstage in Nuala

Fatal Finds in Nuala

Christmas in Nuala

Passage from Nuala

Rough Time in Nuala

Taken in Nuala

High Wire in Nuala

Cold Case in Nuala

Break from Nuala

AN INSPECTOR DE SILVA MYSTERY

STARDUST IN NUALA

HARRIET STEEL

Author's Note and Acknowledgements

Welcome to the twelfth book in the Inspector de Silva mystery series. Like the previous ones, this is a self-contained story but wearing my reader's hat, I usually find that my enjoyment of a series is deepened by reading the books in order and getting to know major characters well. With that in mind, I have included thumbnail sketches of those taking part in this story who have featured regularly in the series.

Several years ago, I had the great good fortune to visit the island of Sri Lanka, the former Ceylon. I fell in love with the country straight away, awed by its tremendous natural beauty and the charm and friendliness of its people. I had been planning to write a detective series for some time and when I came home, I decided to set it in Ceylon in the 1930s, a time when British Colonial rule created interesting contrasts, and sometimes conflicts, with traditional culture. Thus Inspector Shanti de Silva and his friends were born.

I owe many thanks to everyone who helped with this book. John Hudspith was as usual an invaluable editor. Julia Gibbs did a marvellous job of proofreading the manuscript, and Jane Dixon Smith designed another excellent cover and layout for me. My thanks also go to all those readers who have told me they enjoyed the previous books in the series and would like to know what Inspector de Silva and his friends did next. Their enthusiasm has encouraged me to keep writing. Above all, my heartfelt gratitude goes to my husband Roger for his unfailing encouragement and support, to say nothing of his patience when Inspector de Silva's world distracts me from this one.

Apart from well-known historical figures, all characters in this book are fictitious. Nuala is also fictitious although loosely based on the hill town of Nuwara Eliya. Any mistakes are my own.

Characters who appear regularly
in the Inspector de Silva Mysteries

Inspector Shanti de Silva. He began his police career in Ceylon's capital city, Colombo, but in middle age he married and accepted a promotion to inspector in charge of the small force in the hill town of Nuala. Likes: a quiet life with his beloved wife, his car, good food, his garden. Dislikes: interference in his work by his British masters, formal occasions.

Sergeant Prasanna. Nearly thirty and married with a daughter. He's doing well in his job and starting to take more responsibility. Likes: cricket and is exceptionally good at it.

Constable Nadar. A few years younger than Prasanna. Diffident at first, he's gaining in confidence. Married with two boys. Likes: his food, making toys for his sons. Dislikes: sleepless nights.

Jane de Silva. She came to Ceylon as a governess to a wealthy colonial family and met and married de Silva a few years later. A no-nonsense lady with a dry sense of humour. Likes: detective novels, cinema, and dancing. Dislikes: snobbishness.

Archie Clutterbuck. Assistant government agent in Nuala and as such responsible for administration and keeping law and order in the area. Likes: his Labrador, Darcy; fishing, hunting big game. Dislikes: being argued with, the heat.

Florence Clutterbuck. Archie's wife, a stout, forthright lady. Likes: being queen bee, organising other people. Dislikes: people who don't defer to her at all times.

Doctor David Hebden. Doctor for the Nuala area. Under his professional shell, he's rather shy. Likes: cricket. Dislikes: formality.

Emerald Hebden (née Watson). She arrived in Nuala with a touring British theatre company, decided to stay and subsequently married David Hebden. She's a popular addition to local society and a good friend to Jane. Her full story is told in *Offstage in Nuala*.

Sanjeewa Gunesekera. The manager of the Crown hotel and an old friend of Shanti de Silva.

William Petrie. Government agent for the Central Province and therefore Archie Clutterbuck's boss. A charming exterior hides a steely character. Likes: getting things done. Dislikes: inefficiency.

CHAPTER 1

April 1941

The sun was slipping below the hills to the west of Nuala. Crimson and gold suffused the sky, slowly fading with the onset of night. The insistent beat of drums and the rhythmic chant of voices drew nearer. In the crowd of onlookers gathered by the area of sand-strewn grass to the east of the Royal Nuala Cricket Club, the buzz of anticipation swelled. People stood twenty deep, many of them with children hoisted on their shoulders for a better view. The faces of those nearest the front were washed a lurid red by the light of the flaming torches that illuminated the scene.

From his position at the southern end of the film set, Inspector Shanti de Silva surveyed the crowd and the line of policemen tasked with holding it back. Thanks to the number of reinforcements he had called in from Hatton and other police stations further afield, everything was going well, but it would be a relief when the evening was over and everyone went home. Crowds, especially ones as large as this, were unpredictable things.

The area of sand-covered grass had been made to look like a palace courtyard surrounded by stone pillars. The entablature they supported was painted with lurid images of deities and demons, and to the right-hand side there was an entrance punched in a massive arch. De Silva was impressed that the edifice looked so real when it wasn't made of stone at all but of wood, metal, papier-mâché, and paint. No doubt the torchlight helped with the deception.

The area beyond the entrance into the archway was lost in shadow, but soon figures leapt and gyrated into sight. The drumming and chanting grew so loud that de Silva's ears throbbed. Finally a beam of light illuminated the archway and the whole procession came into view. Behind an advance guard of dancers with painted faces and wild hair, swayed a gilded palanquin carried on the shoulders of six men, their bare, powerfully muscled torsos gleaming with oil. They headed for the northern side of the courtyard and carefully set the palanquin down.

A hush fell over the crowd as the palanquin's occupant stepped out. He was a tall man, dressed in a full-length black robe embroidered with gold symbols and stars. He carried a staff tipped with more gold and wore a headdress of feathers dyed scarlet and black. A black mask rendered hideous by a lolling blood-red tongue, white fangs, and bulging bloodshot eyes hid his face. He walked over to the altar where a body covered from head to toe in a magnificent gold cloth lay on a bier, and barked a command. The dancers grew still. All eyes were on him as in a harsh voice that sent a shudder through de Silva's frame, he began to speak.

* * *

It had all started a few weeks previously when the film company arrived in Nuala from Bombay. They came to shoot a drama based on the legend of the Maha Kola Sanni, the demon who had wreaked havoc in one of the kingdoms of ancient Ceylon. De Silva knew the legend well. It told of how a king returned from a long journey to find that his wife was expecting a child. Convinced that the baby wasn't his, he sentenced her to death. But before she died, she gave birth to a baby boy. When he grew to manhood, he wanted revenge for his mother's death, so he took the form of a demon and killed the king, devouring him and spreading disease and disaster throughout his lands. Afterwards, he gathered lumps of soil and fashioned more demons to do his bidding. Each of them was made responsible for a particular disease.

'Dashed nuisance,' his boss Archie had muttered gruffly when he'd called de Silva up to the Residence to tell him that the film company was coming. 'I don't know what all the excitement's about, but William Petrie thinks the project's a good thing. I suppose these film johnnies are paying a steepish amount of money in return for our cooperation and much of it will be used to benefit the area. Petrie also believes it might encourage other projects to come our way. As for my wife, she's been full of it. I understand that the chap in charge who owns the company goes by the name of Dev Khan, and he's pretty well known in the Bombay film world.'

Even though de Silva presumed that a fair amount of the burden of providing this cooperation that Archie referred to was going to fall on him, he was prepared to believe that if William Petrie, Archie's own boss and the government agent for the Kandy region, was in favour of the project, then there must be some value in it.

Exactly how the legend was to be used in film's plot had been something of a mystery at first. Understandably, the filmmakers didn't want too much revealed until the film received its first showing, but the scene tonight with a devil dance being performed and the tall actor dressed as a demonic high priest indicated that an illness needed to be cast out. Jane had managed to find out more.

'Jayasena says the story is about a king whose stepson poisons him in an attempt to seize power. He's helped by his mother, the queen. At the outset everyone believes their story that the king has been made ill by the demon Maha as punishment for a crime he's committed, but in the end, the truth is revealed. The king is brought back to life, the queen and her son are punished, and the king marries again. Dev Khan plays the role of the king, and his wife Sunita plays the queen.'

De Silva wasn't sure that the story deserved to be treated as such a big secret. It sounded pretty standard fare to him, but then what did he know? Jane was the cinema expert. Most of the films that came to the cinema in Nuala were British made anyway, so he knew very little about what came out of India. What did surprise him, however, was that Jayasena had taken an interest. He'd never thought of their sensible, longest-serving member of staff, the only one he trusted to drive his beloved Morris, as being interested in films or gossip.

'How on earth does Jayasena know all this?'

'He met some of the drivers from the film crew in a bar in town.'

De Silva raised an eyebrow. 'And I don't expect their boss would be happy if he heard about their loose tongues.'

'Don't worry. I told Jayasena not to talk to anyone else.'

'I suppose that'll have to be good enough.'

Most of the scenes that were being filmed in Nuala were conducted on closed sets, but the filmmakers had accepted that would be virtually impossible in the case of the one being filmed tonight as it needed a large amount of space in the open air. Accordingly, in return for Archie Clutterbuck's official assurance that the crowds would be kept under control, they had agreed to allow spectators. They'd also stressed that they didn't want any photographs of the scene appearing in the newspapers, so journalists and photographers were expressly banned.

For de Silva, the filming had already been the cause of

considerable disruption. On several occasions the filmmakers had wanted parts of town closed, and with only Sergeant Prasanna and Constable Nadar to support him, he'd had to call in other forces to help. But there were disadvantages to that. He never minded asking a favour of his old friend Inspector Singh at Hatton, but he wasn't on such familiar terms with all the other chiefs of police in the region, and some of the men they'd sent had been so starstruck that they'd needed a stiff lecture to keep them focused on the job in hand. Even Prasanna and Nadar hadn't been immune to being thrown off-beam by the excitement, so the prospect of controlling the large crowds that would be likely to come tonight to watch the big scene, to say nothing of spotting and sending away any journalists and photographers who tried to join them, had caused him a few sleepless nights. Still, the evening had certainly turned out to be exciting. It would be something to remember, and best of all – he surveyed the intact police cordon – so far there had been no trouble.

The high priest's speech ended and the drumming resumed. As their sticks rained down on leather stretched taut over the tops of their gourd-shaped instruments, the drummers sang an eerily monotonous tune. Dressed in scarlet and blue costumes with short, wide skirts that flared out over tight leggings, the dancers began to whirl and stamp, spreading their legs and bouncing on the soles of their feet to make themselves look even more threatening than before. Their faces were hidden by scarlet masks, and long, pale ribbons dangled from their ornate scarlet and gold headdresses. The ribbons lashed the air as the dancers moved; the silver bells attached to their anklets jingled. A powerful smell of incense invaded de Silva's nostrils. The assault on his senses was beginning to make him dizzy. He blinked and shook his head then closed his eyes for a few seconds.

When he opened them, the high priest had raised

a goblet above his head. Light sparkled on its jewel-encrusted surface as he called for the evil spirits to leave the body of the king on the bier. Involuntarily, de Silva held his breath. If he had been asked at any other time, he would have said that the old beliefs were just stories made up to frighten the gullible and cause a delicious frisson of terror in the rest, but the incense, the drumming, the music, the bells, and the wave of tension rolling over the crowd were so powerful that it was hard to quell the surge of primeval fear that threatened to grip him. He dug his fingernails into his palms and fought it down, wondering if any of his fellow policemen were enduring a similar struggle. In particular, he hoped that Prasanna and Nadar wouldn't disgrace his little force.

Time seemed to stretch out in an endless stream then the king's body stirred. Slowly the gold cloth fell away as he rose to a seated position. The murmur of excitement grew louder, and de Silva sensed that the whole crowd, as well as the cast on set, were willing him to recover. As his face was revealed, a shout went up from the cast. 'The King! The King lives!'

Then a louder voice boomed through a megaphone. 'Cut!'

Relieved, de Silva felt air fill his lungs once more. Now all he had to do was get the crowds safely away.

CHAPTER 2

'What an evening!'

De Silva sank into his favourite armchair in the drawing room at Sunnybank and stroked Bella, who had immediately jumped onto his lap. 'You certainly wouldn't have liked it,' he told the little black cat. 'There would have been far too much noise.'

'But you must admit it was exciting to watch,' said Jane.

'Oh, I'll give you that, but policing it was quite a headache.'

'Well, everything seemed to go well to me. I thought the crowd was very well behaved, and when I left with the Hebdens and the Applebys, people were going on their way without any fuss.'

He had been glad that Jane had watched the filming with their good friends Doctor Hebden and his wife Emerald, and that the Applebys had been there too. George Appleby was an imposing fellow. His six-foot-four frame and broad shoulders made it unlikely that anyone would cause trouble for his party.

'Do you think you'll be called on to help again?' asked Jane.

'I don't know. Archie's asked me up to the Residence tomorrow. I hope I'll find out then.' He rolled his shoulders and shifted his weight in his chair. Bella arched her back and gave a small miaow of protest then purred and settled again as he scratched her behind the ears.

'When this is all over, I expect people will miss the excitement,' said Jane. 'Still there's the film to look forward to. Won't it be fun to see Nuala on the big screen.'

'I suppose it will.'

'I hope it won't be too long before they show it here, but the cinema is rather small. I expect it will come to Kandy first. We should take a trip to see it there.'

'Let's think about it nearer the time,' said de Silva. Once all the film was on celluloid rather than in the streets of his hometown, he might remember the disruption it had brought in its wake with greater equanimity. At the moment, he was looking forward to the film company being a thing of the past.

Gently, he put Bella down. 'I don't think I'll bother with a nightcap. Best to get straight off to bed. It won't be long before it's time to wake up again.'

'Are you sure? You've not even had anything to eat this evening, have you?'

'Fortunately, I have. There was a meal for anyone who wanted it after the filming ended. That chap Ashok Mehta, Dev Khan's personal assistant, took the police contingent under his wing and made sure no one went hungry. There were several large tents set up and we ate in one of those.'

'That was very thoughtful of him. What were you given to eat?'

'Rice with a vegetable and chickpea curry. The servers also brought baskets of naan piled up as high as – as Mount Lavinia.' He demonstrated with his hands wide apart.

'I hope you didn't eat too much of the naan.'

'But I'd worked hard all evening.' De Silva pulled a face.

Jane laughed. 'I'll take that as confirmation that you did.' She paused. 'You approve of this young man Ashok, don't you?'

'Yes, he's an excellent organiser and very easy to work

with.' Over the weeks the film company had been in Nuala, de Silva had habitually dealt with their requests through Ashok. He was a charming, good-looking young man, tall and trim with a shrewdly humorous expression in his dark-brown eyes.

'I hope his boss appreciates him,' said Jane.

'Why do you say that?'

'Oh, I hear Dev Khan has a reputation for being very demanding.'

'Is that another of Jayasena's pearls of wisdom?'

Jane smiled. 'Yes.'

De Silva chuckled. 'As you may imagine, Prasanna and Nadar thoroughly enjoyed themselves this evening. I expect it won't be long before there's a story around town that they were fraternising with the stars.'

'And would that be true? If you all had dinner with Dev and Sunita Khan, I shall be extremely jealous, you know.'

'It wasn't quite that grand, although I was introduced to a few of the actors who play the less important roles.' He grinned. 'But the ladies who take the parts of the palace's dancing girls seemed to be making the younger policemen feel welcome.'

Jane raised an eyebrow. 'Not too welcome I hope.'

'Oh, there was nothing improper, I'm sure. It was all innocent fun.' He smiled. 'I last saw Prasanna and Nadar being taught a folk dance. Of course all I wanted to do was to come home to my darling wife, so I left them to it.'

'Flatterer,' said Jane with a laugh. 'I'm sure it was inno-cent. I was only joking.'

She scooped Bella up. 'Time you were off to the kitchen for the night, young lady. I wonder where your brother Billy's got to. I hope we don't have to send out a search party before we can go to bed.'

They never let the cats roam at night. The risk of them meeting a predator in the darkness was too great. Luckily, that night Jane found Billy already in the kitchen lapping up a saucer of milk that the cook had left out. Bella ran to share it and Jane closed the door on them and returned to the drawing room. After checking that the bungalow was safely locked up, the de Silvas went to bed.

But demons danced through Shanti's dreams, and he slept fitfully, envious of Jane who slumbered peacefully at his side. At dawn he woke for the fourth time and saw light filtering around the edges of the curtains. So as not to wake her, he climbed cautiously out of bed, found his dressing gown and slippers, and went quietly out of the bedroom to the hall. When he opened the kitchen door, Billy and Bella ran out to meet him. Together they went into the drawing room where he drew back the curtains and opened the garden door to let them out. A draught of cold air blew in. Thrusting his hands into the pockets of his dressing gown, he watched the cats dash off to explore, Billy a few yards in front as usual.

He pulled the door to, leaving just enough room for them to come back in again then turned up the collar of his dressing gown to warm his neck. Jane often teased him that he didn't know what real cold was, but however hot the weather in the day, there was always a chill at dawn. He thought of his dreams last night. It was strange what a profound effect the scene had had on him. He supposed it was a tribute to the film company. The film looked as if it would be an exciting one. He was glad, however, that the light of day was already driving the demons to the edges of his imagination. He was also not sorry that the film company would soon be gone and life in Nuala could go back to normal.

CHAPTER 3

When de Silva was shown into his boss's study that morning, Archie looked sleepy and bleary-eyed. The mood seemed to have infected his elderly Labrador, Darcy, too. He thumped his tail wearily but remained stretched out like a furry black rug beside his master's chair.

'Bit of a late night,' said Archie a touch sheepishly. 'Mrs Clutterbuck insisted we accept the Khans' invitation to have a drink with them at the Crown after the filming was over.'

De Silva smiled inwardly at the mental image of Archie and Florence partying with the stars. He was sure Florence would have enjoyed it, and this morning's hangover gave the impression that Archie had enjoyed it too.

Archie cleared his throat. 'Now, I expect you'd like to know what's happening next. Dev Khan told me he's pretty sure there'll be no need to do anything more to last night's scene. With all the work that policing it entailed, I imagine you're relieved to hear it.'

'I have to admit, I am.'

'By the way, good show yesterday. I think we can be proud of the way we handled things.'

Used to Archie claiming credit that was not always his due, de Silva murmured a tactful nothing.

'Anyway, now they only need to get a few more daylight scenes in the can.'

De Silva suppressed a smile. He wondered if that was an expression Archie had learnt last night.

'But they'll be filmed in Colombo, so we're not involved. The film crew are packing up today, ready to head off there. The Khans plan to stay on at the Crown to have a bit of a rest before following them. In any case, you're off duty.' He paused. 'Oh, but just one more thing. You might pay a visit to the cricket club. I'd like to be sure the film crew leave the site as they found it.'

'Of course.'

* * *

No pressing jobs awaited him at the police station, so de Silva decided to go straight up to the cricket club. Even if the film crew was still at work, he could find out whether they had done a decent job so far. In any case it was a pleasant day for a drive, and after his disturbed night, a spell in the fresh air would do him good.

The road that led up to the cricket club was in good condition, but beyond the clubhouse there was only a rough grassy track. Presumably the film company's vehicles had coped with it, but he was unwilling to risk damaging the Morris's suspension, so when he reached the clubhouse, he parked there as he'd done the previous evening.

Before setting off across the grass, he paused for a moment, turning to look back in the direction he'd come from. There was a fine view of Nuala from the hill where the cricket club was situated. At the heart of the town, the bazaar was a patchwork of many colours. Beyond it and slightly to his left, the stone tower of St George's church shimmered in the midday heat. The Residence wasn't far away in the same direction; he shaded his eyes to make out its two-storeyed white frontage. The Town Hall and the Crown were also substantial and stood out from the other buildings. Further to his left and beyond the sprawl of modest houses where some of the locals lived was a large area dotted with trees. That was where the leafy streets lined with the comfortable homes of colonial officers and the wealthier locals were, amongst them his and Jane's bungalow, Sunnybank. Over to his right was the racecourse, and beyond it all, the hills with their emerald cloak of tea plantations.

He took a last look then picked up his cap from the passenger seat, put it on, and set off. As he passed the cricket pitch, two groundsmen were pushing a large metal roller over the neatly cropped turf, and workmen were painting the wooden railings that ran across the front of the pavilion. The dome of its white clock tower had recently been refurbished and its new lead cladding sparkled in the sunshine.

He left the club behind and struck out across the grass. Clouds of cream and brown butterflies rose on either side of him. As he passed a small clump of trees, he saw a flash of shiny blue-black plumage. A bird flew out of one tree and into another then settled on a branch. It shuffled along, cocking its head, and trilling staccato bursts of a whistling song. De Silva recognised it as a drongo. It was a crow-like bird; one of the few that came to the Sunnybank garden that was bold enough to stand its ground when Billy and Bella appeared on the scene.

At the site where the filming had taken place the previous night, all that was left to show where the crowds had assembled was trampled grass. The set for the palace courtyard where the devil dancing scene had taken place was almost gone too. With a great deal of shouting of orders from a foreman, workmen were dismantling the last of it, manoeuvring huge painted flats onto trucks. Metal poles rang as they were thrown onto piles, and the thick layer of sand that had covered the grass was being briskly dispersed by a line of men moving across it with brooms. Here and there, flocks of birds swooped down and strutted about, squabbling, and pecking at the ground. All the hammering in and subsequent pulling up of posts and other equipment would have exposed a good crop of worms and insects for them to feast on.

De Silva went over to speak to the foreman who paused briefly in his task.

'You're making good progress.'

The man wiped the back of his hand across his damp forehead. 'Thank you, sahib.' He gestured to the tents where de Silva and the other policemen had dined the previous evening. They were surrounded by an encampment of smaller ones, as well as wooden caravans, and a few temporary-looking buildings. 'All that is going next.'

'I see. I'd like to speak to Ashok Mehta. Do you know where I can find him?'

The man pointed to a group of tents. 'He might be over there.'

De Silva thanked him and walked on in search of Ashok. The first few tents he looked into were empty, but then he came to one where two people were talking inside. The entrance flap was closed, and he was about to call out when what he heard made him hold back.

'Don't you see,' a man was saying in a low, urgent tone. 'If we do nothing, he'll never let us be free to make a life of our own.'

A woman's voice answered but her words were too muffled for de Silva to make them out. He watched as the shadows the couple cast on the side of the tent drew closer to each other and merged in an embrace. The man spoke again, and the woman replied but their voices were very soft now. Perhaps the man wasn't Ashok, thought de Silva, but if he was, this was hardly the time to disturb him.

He was debating whether to walk away and come back later when the tent flap opened. The young woman who emerged recoiled at the sight of him. Her hand went to her throat and clutched the neck of the white blouse that she wore under her red and gold sari. She had a pretty face framed by long, silky dark hair. Her skin was a warm brown and she was slender with a graceful air.

'I'm sorry,' he said. 'I didn't mean to frighten you. I'm looking for Ashok Mehta.'

The young woman pointed to the tent. For a moment she looked as if she might speak, but then without a word she walked swiftly away, her sari rippling in the breeze. De Silva watched her go, then went over to the tent flap. He stepped back as it was abruptly pulled aside, and Ashok nearly crashed into him.

'Inspector de Silva!' The misery in the young man's expression was quickly replaced by a strained smile. 'Were you looking for me?' he asked a little awkwardly.

De Silva decided it was best not to comment on what he'd just heard. Whatever the problem between the young man and his lady friend, he didn't want to add embarrassment to his distress.

'I was, but merely to see how the packing up is going and if you needed any help. I met your foreman on the way over here. He told me these tents are to come down next.'

'Yes. It's good of you to offer your help, but we have everything under control.' Seeming to have swiftly recovered his composure, Ashok gestured to the inside of the tent where there was a large table piled up with stacks of files and papers. 'My office. I still have a few matters to finish off before everything's packed away and sent off to Colombo. Once that's done, my base will be at the Crown with the Khans until they leave Nuala.'

He glanced past de Silva, who turned to see an elderly man with a glum expression on his lined face approaching. He was short with close-cropped, grizzled hair.

Ashok nodded a greeting. 'How are you getting on, Naseer?'

'Most of Dev's trunks are packed. They'll be ready to load in an hour or two.'

'Good. I'll arrange for the transport.'

'Thank you.' The elderly man hurried away at a surprising speed considering his bad limp. It gave him an awkward rolling gait.

Ashok looked at his watch. 'I have a few minutes to spare. May I offer you some refreshment? The catering staff have begun to pack up their equipment, but I expect they could find us some tea or a glass of Elephant ginger beer if you'd prefer it.'

'I don't want to hold you up.'

'You won't. I want to go over and see how they're getting on.' He smiled. 'Anyway it's the least I can do when you've worked so hard to help us. The way you and your men kept those crowds under control was impressive, and as far as I've been able to gather, no articles about the event or photographs of it have turned up in the newspapers. Inquisitive journalists are a big problem in our line of work. Dev and Hari Bedu, our director, would be very unhappy if the papers managed to report on the big scene before the film came out. Apparently, a few photographers did catch shots of the family and some of their guests on their way into the Crown later. I expect they'll be published somewhere, but that's not a problem.'

'Well, if you're sure you can spare the time, a ginger beer would be most welcome.'

'Then let's go.'

'How did your friend Naseer injure his leg?' asked de Silva as they strolled in the direction of the refreshment tents.

'It was crushed by a cartwheel when he was young. He was lucky not to lose it. He once told me it was thanks to Dev that he survived at all. He was unable to work, and Dev helped him. They both grew up in one of the slum areas of Bombay and met as children. Although Naseer looks older, they're about the same age. Naseer's worked as Dev's dresser for all the years Dev's been in the film business.'

'And I gather Dev's been very successful in it. I was most impressed with what I saw last night,'

'Yes, he has. In his youth, he worked in one of the cotton mills in Bombay, but he was fascinated by the idea of films. As soon as he could, he got into the business on the bottom rung. Those were the early days when Indian-made films were still new.'

They'd reached the main refreshment tent and Ashok led the way inside. Without the cast members from the previous evening, many of whom had still been in their costumes, to supply an exotic touch, the place looked drab. Instead of the soft glow of candles and oil lamps, the only light came from some of the tent flaps that had been rolled up, but despite that, the air was stuffy and there was a stale smell of day-old cooking. Men dressed in loincloths were carrying huge nets bulging with cauldrons, pots, pans, and other kitchen equipment on their backs to waiting trucks. Ashok stopped one of them as he returned and told him to bring them two bottles of ginger beer and some snacks. 'It might be more pleasant to have them outside,' he remarked when they arrived. Gladly, de Silva followed him to a spot in the shade of a tree and they sat down on a log.

'Help yourself to samosas,' said Ashok, pointing to the plate of tasty-looking little triangles of fried pastry that he'd set on the ground. De Silva thanked him and ate one, washing it down with some of the ginger beer. It was a little warm, but its sharp taste was always refreshing.

'How did your boss climb the ladder then?' he asked, brushing a few pastry crumbs from his chin.

'At first, he only managed to find small parts in films, but then he started to be given more important roles. When he was thirty, he married a wealthy widow. With her money, he began to realise his ambition to produce films of his own, not just star in other people's. That was twenty years ago.'

Ashok took a swig of his ginger beer and fell quiet.

'What does his family consist of now?' asked de Silva when the silence had gone on for a few moments.

'As you may have gathered, it's one of his stepsons, Raj, who plays the crown prince. He and his brother Salman are the widow's children by her first husband. She and Dev then had a daughter. Raj and Salman were very young when their mother married Dev. He adopted them and gave them his name. His daughter Layla has just turned twenty. Sadly, her mother died not long after she was born. Dev married Sunita a few years ago, but there are no more children. Sunita was already successful in her career and although she's ten years younger than Dev, having a child might have been dangerous for her.'

'And how about you? Have you worked for Dev for long?'

'Two years, but I did other jobs in the film industry before that.' The young man fell silent once more. He pulled a leaf off a low branch of the tree and rolled it between a finger and thumb. It stained his skin green as he crushed it to a pulp. Frowning, he muttered something inaudible. He seemed to have forgotten de Silva was there.

De Silva was tempted to offer sympathy. Presumably Ashok's problem was to do with the pretty girl he'd seen coming out of the tent. But then he thought better of it. The young man might not welcome an intrusion from someone who was virtually a stranger to him. Anyway, Ashok had work to do. Perhaps that would distract him from his troubles in love.

He finished his ginger beer. 'Many thanks, that was most welcome. I won't keep you any longer. If you find you need me after all, just send a message to the station.'

'That's very kind. I'll remember.'

CHAPTER 4

On his return to town, de Silva was close to the Crown when he saw his friend Sanjeewa Gunesekera, the hotel manager, driving from the opposite direction. Sanjeewa saw him and waved, and as there was very little other traffic, de Silva drew to a halt next to him.

'Have you had lunch?' asked Sanjeewa.

'Not yet, unless you count a ginger beer and a few snacks. I've been up to the cricket club. The film crew are getting ready to move on and Archie Clutterbuck wanted me to check everything will be left in order.'

'And will it?'

'As far as I can tell, yes. Ashok Mehta, Dev Khan's personal assistant, is in charge. He seems very capable. But I'm surprised to see you out at this hour. Aren't you usually at the hotel?'

'I had a meeting at the bank, and it took longer than expected, but I'm off to the hotel now. My lunch is long overdue. If you have room after your snacks and nothing to hurry for, why not join me? It's a while since we caught up.'

A convivial lunch with his old friend was an appealing prospect and de Silva realised that he was hungry. If there was anything new to be dealt with at the station, it would do Prasanna and Nadar no harm to cope without him for a bit. 'Thank you,' he said. 'I'd like nothing better.'

Often, when his friend invited him to lunch, they ate in Sanjeewa's office but after a glance inside, he decreed that it was far too stuffy there and they'd eat in the garden. On the way, he stopped at the reception desk and told them to send a waiter out to where they'd be sitting. 'Oh and tell housekeeping I want my office thoroughly aired before I go back to work.'

As they stepped through the double doors that led from one of the lounges onto the terrace at the back of the hotel, de Silva breathed in the heady perfume of the white rambling rose that covered the walls on either side. The terrace was quiet. Most of the residents had already eaten lunch and gone to their rooms to rest, so it was without interruptions that they reached the quiet spot under a trellised arbour that Sanjeewa had chosen. He plumped down in one of the chairs with a sigh.

'Good. I'm glad I didn't have to stop to chat to any guests. When I'm as hungry as I am now, small talk's a chore.'

'Is that the only time?' asked de Silva with a smile.

His friend shrugged. 'It's part of my job, but I must admit, some guests are more of a pleasure to converse with than others.'

'What about your celebrity guests?'

'All of my guests are celebrities,' said Sanjeewa with a laugh. 'But seriously, I know you mean the Khans. Your boss and his wife were here last night and seemed to be having a good time with them in the bar. I was a little surprised, I must say. You've never mentioned that the Clutterbucks like to let their hair down.'

'That's because I've very rarely seen them do so, and then it's mainly been Archie.'

A waiter arrived with menus and Sanjeewa took charge of ordering their meal.

'Dev Khan hasn't shown much inclination to party whilst he's been with us at the hotel,' he said when the waiter went off to take their order to the kitchen. 'I've noticed that he's careful about how much he drinks. I'm told by that personal assistant of his, Ashok Mehta, that he has heart trouble and takes medication every day. A very pretty nurse by the name of Anne Collins travels with him to see to it that he does. But perhaps on this occasion he was relieved that the big scene went according to plan and wanted to celebrate.'

'I hear he's staying on for a while.'

'Yes, with his family. His wife Sunita who plays the part of the queen in the film, his stepson Raj who plays the crown prince and then another stepson and a daughter from his first marriage to a lady who died some years ago.'

'I haven't come across the last two. Are they not involved with the film?'

'They are, but not on the acting side. The daughter, Layla, has inherited her father's good looks and I think his love of films. She seems to be interested in the designing of costumes and so on. The other stepson is called Salman. I haven't managed to work him out. He's a writer and has apparently been involved in the screenplay for the film, but it would be hard to imagine anyone who appears to derive so little enjoyment from a job that I'm sure many would envy.'

'I wonder why that is.'

'Hard to say as an outsider, but my guess is that Dev Khan isn't an easy man to live up to. He dotes on his daughter, but I've heard him speak very harshly to his stepsons. He wouldn't be the first man to set different standards for boys and girls, and of course Raj and Salman aren't his own flesh and blood, but he may also think that if he had to fight to get on in the world, as I believe he did, others should have to do the same. Raj seems to cope, although I suspect he drinks more than is good for him, but I have the impression that Salman is more sensitive and struggles with Dev's criticisms.'

'I understand both boys were very young when their mother died.'

'Yes, I believe they were, so Dev is in effect the only father figure they've ever known. But who told you that?'

'Ashok Mehta. Up until now our conversations have been mostly about business, but we had quite a long chat up at the cricket club today.'

'A likeable young man. Capable of greater things than he's doing now.'

'You think so?'

Sanjeewa nodded but before he had time to continue, three waiters came in their direction carrying trays laden with cutlery, plates, glasses, and steaming serving dishes.

'Ah good, here's lunch,' said Sanjeewa, rubbing his hands together.

As the waiters descended on the table, a collared dove that had been hunting for insects in the dry leaves under a nearby bush, jerked up its head and flew away.

A crisp white cloth was spread, and the table quickly laid. Soon, de Silva was looking with pleasure at an array of delicious food: beetroot curry, fish roasted with coconut, a large dish of rice, a bowl of pennywort salad mixed with chopped onions, coconut and spices, and a pile of perfectly charred roti. Sanjeewa raised his glass of beer. 'To your good health. Tuck in.'

'What did you mean about Ashok Mehta?' asked de Silva a few minutes later when the worst of his hunger pangs had been assuaged.

Sanjeewa reached for a spoon and ladled some more coconut relish onto his rice. 'I'm not sure that being Dev Khan's assistant has great prospects. When Dev goes, the business will presumably pass to his children. No chance of moving up the ladder there.'

'What about his wife?'

'I've no idea, but they've only been married a few years.' Sanjeewa looked around him and lowered his voice. 'Between ourselves, the relationship is a stormy one. At one time last night, I thought that the filming might not proceed. The two of them had a big argument in Sunita's suite – they've taken one each which is probably a wise idea. If they're not getting on, they have some space between them. The argument wasn't the first they've had since they arrived. I don't know what it was about, but a valuable vase and a mirror were broken. One of the maids who was passing heard shouting and then the sound of breakages, but she was afraid to go in. She ran down to find me and I thought I'd better investigate in case either of the Khans were injured, but by the time I reached the room, there was no sign of Dev, and Sunita had retreated to her bedroom. The maid who travels with her was on her hands and knees picking up broken china and glass from the floor. From the resigned expression on her face, I guessed that she was used to it.'

He shrugged. 'This morning Dev came down alone to breakfast with a face like thunder, and Sunita's maid rang saying her mistress wanted breakfast served in her suite. Fortunately for all concerned though, before I left the hotel I saw them having coffee together on the terrace as if nothing had happened, but she's a demanding lady and he likes his own way too. I think I'll be lucky if their visit comes to an end without any more of the hotel's property being smashed up.'

'It must be an exhausting way to live,' observed de Silva.

'It seems that way to you and me, but maybe the acting temperament is different, and they thrive on it.'

'Perhaps you're right.' De Silva crumpled up his napkin and put it beside his empty plate. 'Thank you for an excellent meal. A treat that I wasn't expecting when I came to work this morning.'

'I'm glad you approved. Our chef will be pleased. Would you like some tea before you go?'

De Silva glanced at his watch. If he stayed, it would be almost time to go home by the time he reached the station but perhaps he'd allow himself a little longer to relax. It wasn't every day that one had to deal with a visit from a film company and he felt he could congratulate himself on a good job done.

'I don't want to hold you up.'

'You won't.' Sanjeewa stood up. 'I'll go and catch the eye of one of our waiters.' But he hadn't gone far when a bellboy coming from the direction of the hotel stopped him. They spoke for a few moments then Sanjeewa returned to the table.

'I'm afraid I have to go. A problem with one of the guests that needs my attention.'

'Never mind, another time.' De Silva got to his feet and clapped his old friend on the shoulder. 'Good to see you and thank you again.'

'It was a great pleasure. If you don't need to hurry away, why don't I have some tea brought out for you anyway?'

It was very pleasant in the hotel garden. De Silva hesitated a moment then nodded. 'I think my duties can spare me for a little longer. That would be most kind.'

The tea arrived and he sat for another quarter of an hour before deciding that he really should return to the station. He was still some distance from the main terrace when he noticed the Khans sitting at one of the tables. Dev wore a soft-collared white shirt with a royal blue and crimson silk cravat. Without the heavy makeup he'd worn when he played the king in the film, he looked much more hand-some, and his grey hair was cut in a sleek western style. He seemed relaxed but his wife, striking in a dress with a bold, black-and-white geometric pattern, was talking volubly. Her dark hair was pinned up in an elaborate style and her eyes were hidden behind outsized sunglasses. The two young men at the table – de Silva recognised one of them from the filming as Raj and assumed the other was Salman – presented a contrast. Raj looked as relaxed as Dev did and was also dressed in expensive-looking casual clothes. He was flamboyantly handsome with curly dark hair. But his brother, if it was him, was more sombrely dressed and his thin, sensitive face had a sad expression. He'd pushed his chair away from the table as if he wanted no part in the conversation.

It was the occupant of the last chair, however, who interested de Silva the most. She was the young woman who had been talking in private with Ashok Mehta up at the cricket club that morning. If she was Dev's daughter Layla, as de Silva guessed she was, it explained why Ashok had spoken to her as he did in the tent. The "he" that he'd referred to must be Dev. A man like him was unlikely to accept an employee as a suitable match for his daughter, especially when he doted on her.

Perhaps Ashok was trying to persuade Layla to run away with him, but she was uncertain. It would be understandable. She had a lot to lose. De Silva doubted there was much chance of a happy outcome to the relationship. It was no wonder Layla had looked alarmed when she bumped into him coming out of the tent. A witness to the scene was bound to be unwelcome. Gossip had a way of spreading. He hesitated then decided to leave by a more circuitous route in case seeing him embarrassed her.

The area he walked through was prettily landscaped with walls that supported climbing roses and jasmine. He drank in the heady scents as he passed then, finally on the drive, stopped to inspect the pond. The fountain in the middle of it rained down jets of water, the droplets sparkling like new pins in aquamarine cloth.

Everything looked immaculate. His friend Sanjeewa

might give the impression of always being relaxed and affable, but he ran a tight ship. It wouldn't do for the Crown's privileged guests to see a weed or an untrimmed hedge or shrub.

* * *

Back at the station, Nadar was behind the counter in the public room and there was no sign of Prasanna.

'He's gone to the bazaar, sir,' said Nadar when de Silva asked. 'You said you wanted us to keep an eye on what's going on there.'

'So I did.'

With the extra work that having the film company in Nuala had entailed he had forgotten, but recently there had been a string of petty thefts in the bazaar, a problem that needed to be firmly discouraged. 'Anything else to report?'

'No, sir.'

Perhaps another cup of tea was in order? He told Nadar to bring him one and headed for his office.

Ten minutes later he was putting the final touches to a report on a recent incident involving two warring neighbours, one of whom claimed the other had stolen some of his chickens, when he heard a knock. He called out to come in and Nadar appeared. 'Mrs de Silva is here, sir. Shall I show her in?'

'By all means.'

He straightened his tie and smiled as Jane came into the room. 'Hello, my love. This is an unexpected pleasure.'

'I hope I'm not interrupting anything important.'

'Not at all. Just a routine report.' He rolled his eyes. 'Neighbours who are always fighting over something. I've warned them that next time, I'll fine them both for disturbing the peace.'

'Oh dear.'

He shrugged. 'They have only themselves to blame.'

'I came into town to have a fitting for the new dress I'm having made at Bentleys.'

'Do we have a special occasion coming up?'

'David and Emerald Hebden are having a little party for Olivia. It will be her first birthday. I thought that as her godmother, I ought to make a special effort. Anyway, the dress will come in useful for Florence's next do at the Residence.'

De Silva grinned. 'Very practical.'

'My appointment's done and I've no more shopping, so rather than find a rickshaw or a taxi to take me home, I thought I'd come and see if you're ready to finish work.'

De Silva thought of the leisurely lunch he'd enjoyed, but it didn't happen every day. He silently vowed to make an early start in the morning. 'Well, I'll let you tempt me,' he said.

'Good, shall we have a walk by the lake? We haven't been down there for a long time and it's a wonderful place from which to see the sunset.'

'An excellent idea. I'll just have a word with Nadar and Prasanna if he's back and then we'll be off.'

* * *

As they drove to the lake, he told her about his lunch with Sanjeewa.

'What a shame a family that outwardly seems to have everything is unhappy,' she said. 'I'm sure Sanjeewa's right about Dev Khan expecting a lot from his stepsons because he had to overcome obstacles as a young man, but it's sad, when listening to Salman and encouraging him might produce a better result than criticising him. I don't expect having a volatile stepmother helps either.'

'Ah well, none of this is our problem I'm glad to say. We can enjoy the sunset and forget about the Khans. They'll soon be gone.'

Down at the lake, families and groups of friends strolled about. It was a popular place for watching the sunset, but for now the sun's rays were still sparkling on the waters, dusting it with flecks of gold. A clutch of brightly coloured rowing boats was pulled up on the sand at the little beach at one end. Children ran in and out of the water, laughing and shouting. A few had swum out, their dark heads bobbing in the water, sleek as seals.

Further away, a small team of ponies stood close to the shoreline or in the shallows. They seemed to enjoy being by the lake. Presumably flies troubled them less and they also liked to drink the sweet water. Over the years, there had been complaints from the stall holders selling snacks and coconuts that the ponies tried to raid the stalls, but de Silva's efforts to move them on had never been entirely successful. Anyway, in his view, humans ought to be content to share the world with other living things, no matter the occasional inconvenience.

Arm in arm, he and Jane completed a circuit of the lake then stopped and sat down on one of the benches in the old kiosk close to where the rowing boats were moored.

'What a lovely smell of new wood,' remarked Jane. 'I think the floor must have been replaced recently. I don't remember it being in such good condition. Shanti?'

'Mm?'

'You weren't listening, were you?'

'I'm sorry, I've just noticed a young man over there. I saw him up at the Crown and I think he's Salman Khan. I can't imagine what he's doing down here.'

'Waiting to see the sunset as we are?'

'He can do that from the Crown.'

'Perhaps he just wants some time on his own.'

'I hope that doesn't mean the Khans are having another fight. Poor Sanjeewa was hoping not to lose any more ornaments.'

The young man leant against the bonnet of the black Jaguar he had driven up in, staring at the lake, but frequently he turned his head to scan the road from town. As the sun dipped towards the horizon, rinsing the water with orange light, he started to pace up and down, kicking at loose stones in his way.

'I wonder who he's waiting for,' said Jane.

'Whoever it is, I don't think they're coming. But at least he has a very enviable car.'

'Shanti, that's not very sympathetic of you.' Jane shook her head.

'I only meant that being rich and unhappy must have more consolations than being unhappy and poor.'

She grabbed his hand. 'Oh look! We're missing the sunset.'

They watched as the shimmering sun descended and the colour of the sky turned from russet and gold to indigo thinly streaked with carmine where earth and sky met. When de Silva looked back to see if the Jaguar was still there, it and Salman Khan had gone.

CHAPTER 5

And so an uneventful day came and went. De Silva grew hopeful that he had heard the last of the warring neighbours and their chickens. He hadn't been long at the station the following morning when he received a telephone call from Sanjeewa. Normally so calm and urbane, his friend sounded surprisingly agitated. De Silva listened carefully, as Sanjeewa explained that there had been another argument between the Khans. As before, Dev Khan had stormed out but this time, he'd headed for his car and was driving away at speed when he skidded on the gravel and ran into one of the gardeners who was brushing up leaves near the gateway to the road.

'Is the gardener badly hurt?'

'He's in pain and still shocked. I've called Doctor Hebden out to have a look at him. He told me to try to keep Darsh calm and as still as possible until he arrives.'

'What about Khan?'

'He's fine physically but mentally about as easy to deal with as a bull elephant with a sore head. I persuaded him with great difficulty to come to one of the lounges. Fortunately, the hotel's not very busy, and I've impressed upon the staff who know what's happened that they're not to talk to anyone. With a celebrity like Dev, there's always a risk of journalists sniffing a story. If at all possible, I don't want other guests finding out what's happened either.

Scandal makes for bad publicity. Equally, I know it's only right that Dev Khan makes some kind of restitution.'

De Silva hesitated. It wasn't hard to read Sanjeewa's mind; he was hoping that the matter could be dealt with without a formal charge of dangerous driving. If the gardener was prepared to accept that and was properly compensated, it might be possible, but it was too soon to promise anything. 'I'll be with you shortly,' he said.

'Thank you. Just come to reception and ask them to call me.'

* * *

The lobby at the Crown was quiet, and as far as de Silva was aware, he reached the reception desk without his arrival attracting the curiosity of other guests. He waited there for Sanjeewa to arrive. As his friend walked across the lobby, his face wore his professional smile, but it was strained and there was a furrow between his eyebrows.

'Thank you for getting here so quickly. Darsh is in the staff quarters. Hebden's with him at the moment.'

De Silva followed Sanjeewa out of the lobby and through the green baize door that led to the staff area of the hotel. As they reached the kitchens, wafts of steamy air and the sounds of lunch being prepared drifted out: the clattering of pots and pans, the sputter and hiss of frying and searing, the cacophony of shouted orders, and the whir of fans. De Silva paused briefly to inhale the aromas of roasting meat, spices, and baking, and glimpsed a table where two men stood at an enormous chopping block, their knives flashing through mounds of fresh herbs. At the other end of the table, spices were being ground in mortars and pestles. Some were already prepared and the bowls containing them were a tapestry of rich, earthy colours. A wonderful place, he thought, remembering his recent delicious lunch at the hotel.

The sounds and smells faded as they continued down the corridor until they reached a door to a courtyard with low buildings on either side. They were made of mud brick and roofed with straw, but they looked solid enough and the courtyard was clean and tidy. There were touches of colour in the bright curtains that hung at some of the windows and the painted good luck amulets nailed to many of the doors.

'Darsh is over here,' said Sanjeewa, pointing to one of the doors in the building that formed the back of the courtyard.

They went over to it and entered a tiny lobby with a corridor ahead that had four more doors leading off it. The walls were roughly plastered but the whitewash was clean; the floor was made of compacted earth. Sanjeewa led the way to the far door on the right, opened it and stood back for de Silva to go in.

He was glad to find that the room was also clean and pleasantly cool. Presumably, the sun didn't often shine directly into it. The view through the window was of the narrow lane at the back of the building where there were maintenance sheds and storerooms. There were bunks on the two walls at right angles to the window, each with three tiers.

The gardener, Darsh, lay on the bottom tier of one of them. He let out a yelp and grimaced as Hebden, who sat on the wooden chair beside him, probed his right leg. 'Sorry, old chap. Now, I need to move it about a bit.' He gently manoeuvred Darsh's leg from side to side and this time the gardener endured the treatment with glum stoicism.

'Well done, old chap, that's all satisfactory. Nothing's broken.'

Hebden looked up and nodded to de Silva. 'Good

morning. I'm glad to say the injury isn't as bad as it might have been. As you see, this ankle is badly swollen and there's a lot of bruising, but I have a salve that should help with that. Just to be on the safe side, I'll strap the ankle up and if necessary, it can stay like that for a few weeks, but I'm confident of a good recovery.' He turned to Darsh. 'You'll be as right as rain in no time.'

'Thank you, sahib,' said Darsh weakly.

'Your boss will see to it that you get a few tots of arrack to help with the pain, won't you, Gunesekera?'

A somewhat brighter expression came over Darsh's face.

'I'll send over a pair of crutches. You mustn't put weight on the foot for the time being, do you understand? I'll tell you when it's safe to do so. In the meantime, as much rest as possible.'

He looked around the bare room and then at Sanjeewa. 'Is there somewhere more congenial he can be moved to so that he doesn't have to stare at these walls all day?'

'I'll see what can be arranged.'

'Is there anything you want to ask, de Silva?'

'I'd like Darsh here to tell me in his own words exactly what happened when he was injured.'

'Very well. Gunesekera, shall we wait outside?'

Sanjeewa looked a little reluctant, but he followed Hebden out of the room, leaving de Silva to listen to Darsh's account of the accident. To all intents and purposes, it matched what de Silva had already heard. It was clear to him that Dev Khan had been driving dangerously. 'Who else saw the accident happen?' he asked.

'There were other gardeners around.'

'Can you give me their names?' De Silva got out his notebook and wrote them down as Darsh reeled them off.

'I expect you know that Sahib Khan is an important guest of the hotel,' said de Silva when he had finished. 'Although that doesn't excuse his behaviour. But for now, I'd like to talk to you about your own situation.'

'Will I still be paid my wages while I can't work?'

'I'll talk to your boss and clear that up with him. Do you have a family?'

Darsh shook his head. 'I'm not married, sahib.'

'Is there anyone else who depends on you?'

Again, a shake of the head.

'So, if you continue to be paid until you're well enough to work again, may I take it you're content to leave the matter as it is?'

'Yes, sahib.'

'Thank you. I'll go and speak to your boss.'

Outside, Hebden and Sanjeewa were talking quietly in the courtyard. They stopped and greeted de Silva as he emerged from the building.

'What's the verdict?' asked Hebden.

'His account of the accident is as Sanjeewa outlined. It's clear to me that Dev Khan was driving dangerously but provided Darsh continues to be paid until he recovers, he's prepared to forgive and forget.'

'That's a relief,' said Sanjeewa.

'How much longer are the Khans booked into the hotel for?'

'Another week.'

'Good. At least that gives us a reasonable amount of time to deal with this. I'll need to speak to Archie Clutterbuck and see how he wants to proceed.'

Sanjeewa's mouth turned down. 'What course of action do you think he'll take?'

'Dangerous driving's a serious matter, but if Khan's prepared to admit he was at fault, and Darsh isn't complaining, Archie may be satisfied with giving a warning and a fine. I imagine you'd also appreciate a contribution to the cost of paying Darsh while he can't work.'

Sanjeewa looked doubtful. 'To be honest, that's less important than avoiding bad publicity for the hotel. As for the rest, I know that the law is the law.' He sighed. 'I'll go back and assure Darsh that his wages will be paid.'

* * *

Hebden and de Silva left Sanjeewa to talk to Darsh and returned to the hotel lobby, Hebden to collect what he needed from his car, and de Silva to find Dev Khan.

The lounge that he'd been taken to led off the lobby. Ashok Mehta was with him. He stood up when de Silva came in, but Dev remained in his chair, a sour expression on his handsome face.

'How's the gardener?' asked Ashok.

'Fortunately, I don't think his injury is as bad as it might have been. Given time, Doctor Hebden thinks it will heal satisfactorily.'

'What happens now?'

'I'll have to make a report to Mr Clutterbuck, the assistant government agent. It will be up to him to decide how to proceed, but as I'm sure you're aware, dangerous driving is a serious offence.'

'Dangerous?' exploded Dev. 'The man was in my way.'

With an effort, de Silva suppressed his annoyance. 'Even if that were true, sir, and I understand from the gardener who was knocked down that there are witnesses to the fact that you were driving too fast and swerved off the road without warning, it would be unlikely to be accepted as an excuse for running him down.'

'Who are these witnesses?'

'Until they've been interviewed, I'm not prepared to divulge that.'

'Do you really expect anyone to credit the babbling of a few workmen?' With a snort, Dev jumped from his chair, and stalked to the window. He drummed his fingers on the sill, and Ashok threw de Silva an apologetic glance. 'It might be best if you leave us alone for a few moments,' he said in an undertone.

A knot of anger tightened in de Silva's chest. Khan was insufferably arrogant. He wanted to ask why he assumed the witnesses were workmen. It indicated he'd seen them, but then he decided it might be best to follow Ashok's advice. 'I'll be in the lobby,' he said with as much dignity as he could muster.

He sat down in one of the leather armchairs, picked up a car magazine from the coffee table at his elbow and was trying to distract himself by reading it when there was a commotion at the front entrance. Followed by porters laden with many pieces of expensive-looking luggage, a couple strolled in. The man was on the short side, his stout figure encased in loose white trousers and a tunic that strained over his ample belly. He was balding, and de Silva guessed him to be in his late sixties.

The lady with him might have been a few years younger. She was also stout but taller by half a head. The fine green silk of her sari was thickly embroidered with gold, but if that hadn't attracted attention, her face certainly would have. Adding to the air of confidence with which she carried herself, she had a strong jaw, the eyes of a hawk, a wide mouth with lips painted scarlet, and sharply pencilled-in eyebrows.

At the reception desk, they spoke in Hindi, so de Silva guessed they must be Indian. He didn't understand very much of what was being said, but it wasn't hard to work out that the lady was displeased about something, perhaps the suite they were being offered.

One of the receptionists made a telephone call while the other continued to apologise profusely. De Silva returned to reading his magazine, and when he next looked up, his friend Sanjeewa was with the couple. De Silva felt a pang of sympathy. The lady was doing the majority of the talking and she didn't look much mollified.

'Inspector?'

De Silva turned to see Ashok.

'I'm sorry to have kept you waiting. Mr Khan would be grateful if you'd come back into the lounge.'

'Certainly.' De Silva stood up, wondering if that was really how Ashok's boss had put it. But when they entered the room, he did seem to have simmered down considerably. He gave de Silva a charming smile.

'This has been a most unfortunate business. It may be that I wasn't driving with all the care that I usually do. There were extenuating circumstances, but I won't bore you with them. Suffice to say, I'm extremely relieved to hear that the gardener's not seriously injured.'

There was a silence. De Silva saw Ashok give his boss a meaningful look. Dev returned a sulky one before he carried on.

'Naturally, if there's anything further that I can do to assist, I'll be glad to. I intend to remain in Nuala for another week. You can contact me here if you need to speak to me.'

De Silva had the sensation that the wind had been taken out of his sails. It was clear that it was Ashok's influence that had changed Dev's attitude. The young man had probably anticipated, quite reasonably, that where a man of Dev's status was concerned, an admission that he might have been in the wrong would result at worst in a fine that he could well afford to pay, and at best, in a few words of warning, whereas continuing to deny everything might make matters worse. In the circumstances, de Silva decided that before he took any further action, it would be advisable to speak to Archie. With his aversion to anything that might involve Nuala in a scandal, it was likely he would be keen to settle matters as quickly and quietly as possible. And provided that didn't mean that Darsh suffered an injustice, was there really any harm in it?

'Is that all for the moment, Inspector?' asked Ashok.

'Yes.'

'Thank you.'

Ashok went to the door and stepped out into the lobby. De Silva stood aside to let Dev follow, but when Dev drew level, he paused. De Silva wondered whether he also was going to thank him, but Dev didn't turn to look at him. Instead he muttered something. It sounded like, 'I never forget a face'.

The incident was over in a moment, and Dev walked on to join Ashok, who seemed unaware that anything had happened, but the glacial tone in which the words had been uttered sent a shiver down de Silva's spine.

Once they were all in the lobby, however, Dev was all smiles again. Left alone, de Silva shook his head. The actor could change like a chameleon. He had to admire Ashok for knowing how to handle him. He looked around for his friend Sanjeewa, but he was still busy with his demanding guests. De Silva went to the desk and told one of the receptionists that he was going back to the police station.

'When Mr Gunesekera is free, please let him know he can ring me there.'

CHAPTER 6

On the drive back to the station, it took him a few minutes to shake off the uncomfortable feeling that Dev's words had left him with, but by the time he drew up outside it, he'd regained his equanimity. It was unfortunate if he'd made an enemy of the fellow, but he supposed it went with the job. In any case, what could Dev do to him? It was possible he'd try to speak to Archie before de Silva had the chance to, but although Archie could be irascible at times, he was a fair-minded man. De Silva was confident that he'd want the matter properly dealt with in accordance with the law.

Inside the station, he found the public room empty, but Nadar swiftly appeared from the back.

'Sorry, sir. Prasanna and I were just eating our lunch.'

De Silva sniffed the air and caught the enticing aroma of spices and caramelised onions. 'And very good it smells too.'

'Is everything alright at the hotel, sir?'

He had only given Prasanna and Nadar a brief outline of why Sanjeewa had called, so he explained in greater detail. 'It may all come to nothing,' he concluded, 'but I need to speak to Mr Clutterbuck about it. If he's available, I'll drive up and see him this afternoon. When you've finished your lunch, call the Residence for me. I'm going out to get some lunch myself now.'

'Yes, sir.'

He stepped out into the sunshine once more and headed for the bazaar. For the last few days, the heat had been searing and no rain had fallen. Carts, oxen, and donkeys kicked up eddies of dust from the parched ground. There wasn't a cloud in the hard blue sky and not a tremor of breeze to freshen the air. April was often a particularly hot month. He would be relieved when the monsoon arrived in May.

It occurred to him that it would be advisable for Dev Khan to complete his filming in Colombo before then. Once the rains came, they often turned the dry ground to a quagmire in a matter of a few hours. If Dev knew that, it might be contributing to his shortness of temper, although if it was the case, it was hard to understand why he was staying on in Nuala when he didn't need to. But then Hari Bedu, the director Ashok had mentioned, didn't seem to be around, so perhaps he was down in Colombo getting everything ready and Dev was used to taking it easy when it suited him.

I won't be sorry to see him go, thought de Silva. Convenience never excused injustice, but if, as seemed to be the case, no lasting harm had been done, it was tempting to wish that Archie would decide on a low-key approach to the accident so that Dev and his dangerous driving would no longer be Nuala's problem.

The outskirts of the bazaar were quiet. Local women who did their daily shopping there would already have bought what they wanted and returned home to begin the slow process of grinding fresh spices and chopping vegetables. The curries they made with them would simmer for hours over gentle heat until the flavours merged into appetising dishes.

As de Silva neared the centre of the bazaar, however, the narrow lanes were crowded with people buying their lunch from stalls. He bought some rice and dahl and walked until he found a shady place to sit to one side of a small square. A jacaranda tree, not yet in bloom, cast blue fingers of shadow on the shabby whitewashed wall of the house behind it. A small group of dun-coloured pack donkeys drowsed in the shade, occasionally jerking up their heads to flick away flies. They seemed content enough although they were skinny, with ribs that strained against the hide on their flanks.

At a water pump nearby, a man filled a tin mug and drank then sluiced the remaining water over his head. Droplets glittered in the sunshine. De Silva guessed that he was the owner of the donkeys and might have walked in from one of the villages that morning to bring produce to market.

A woman came out of the doorway to one of the houses, a bundle of washing under her arm. She set it down near the pump then went back into the house and returned with a tin bucket. She pumped water into it then picked out a red blouse from her bundle. When she had wetted it in the bucket, she laid it on a flat stone, soaped it and began to scrub vigorously.

Fascinated by her energy on such a hot afternoon, de Silva almost didn't notice the man who left the house she'd come from. He looked to be about thirty, tall with black hair that curled over his ears, chocolate brown skin, and dark eyes that took on a wary expression when he noticed that de Silva had seen him. Going over to the woman who was now rinsing her blouse, the man bent down and spoke to her briefly. Money changed hands then he straightened up and returned to the house.

De Silva wondered what he was doing there. He looked too well dressed to live in such a modest place. Like the other houses in the square, it was in poor condition, the whitewashed walls peeling and streaked with damp where water looked to have overflowed from broken gutters. The paint on the door and the window frames was peeling and the glass in one of them was badly cracked.

He returned to his meal and was just eating the last few morsels of rice when he spotted a figure in the doorway of the house. He wondered if it was the same man coming out again, but his face was too much in shadow to be sure. If it was him, he must have changed his mind for he went back inside. By the time de Silva left the square, he still hadn't re-emerged.

* * *

'I telephoned the Residence as you asked, sir,' said Nadar when de Silva arrived back at the station. 'They say you are in luck. Mr Clutterbuck is going away tomorrow but he'll see you at half past three this afternoon.'

'Good. Where's Sergeant Prasanna got to?'

'He went to the bazaar again, sir.'

'Ah, good.'

De Silva glanced at the clock on the wall. It was only just past two o'clock and it wouldn't take him long to drive over to the Residence. He had time to write up a report of the interview with Dev and Ashok before he set off. 'I'll be in my office. Bring me a cup of tea, would you?'

'Yes, sir.'

It was stuffy in his office, so he turned on the ceiling fan. Slowly, with a sound like a wheezy old engine cranking into life, its wooden blades gathered speed, but it hardly cooled the hot, sticky air. Still, he consoled himself, April in the hill country was a considerable improvement on the same time of year in Colombo. Outside the window, a small brown bird hopped along the sill, occasionally pecking angrily at the glass. 'You wouldn't want to be in here if you knew how hot it is,' muttered de Silva. Perhaps the little creature had mistaken its reflection for another bird. He tapped on the glass, and it flew away.

There was a knock at the door and Nadar came in. 'Your tea, sir.'

De Silva pushed a pile of papers aside. 'Thank you, put it there.'

Nadar did so, then hovered by the desk. 'Is there anything else, sir?'

'Not at the moment.' De Silva took a closer look at his constable. 'Something you want to ask me?'

The young man cleared his throat. 'Prasanna is back now, sir. May we speak to you about a matter?'

'That sounds ominous. Well, you'd better call him in.'

A few moments later, both young men stood in front of him.

'It is about our pay, sir,' Prasanna said in a rush. 'We and our wives…'

The chair creaked as de Silva leant back and steepled his hands. 'Go on.'

'We and our wives have been speaking about it.'

De Silva guessed that Nadar's wife had raised the subject. He'd heard from Prasanna that she was a forceful lady.

'Our sons grow fast,' said Nadar. 'They need new shoes very often, and schoolbooks. Our home is small. My wife would like a bigger place for us.' He paused for breath before continuing, 'I do my best to work hard, sir. I hope my work is satisfactory.'

He might not be as clever as Sergeant Prasanna, thought de Silva, but Nadar was conscientious and very willing. He smiled. 'I have no complaints.'

Nadar's expression brightened, and he stood taller. 'Thank you, sir.'

'And what do you want to say, Prasanna?'

'Kuveni and I are expecting another baby—'

'Congratulations.'

'Thank you, sir. We are very happy, but it will mean more expense.'

'I see that.'

'Then we humbly ask you to consider our request for an increase in our pay. It has not gone up for three years.'

De Silva frowned. Was it really that long? He should have given it some thought before now.

'A considerable time, I agree. But it's not only my decision, you understand. I'll have to speak to the assistant government agent about it, but I think I can see my way to recommending that your salaries are reviewed.'

'Might you speak to him today, sir?'

De Silva considered the question. If Archie was off on a jolly trip of some kind, he was likely to be in a good mood and more approachable. 'Perhaps.' He lifted the teacup on his desk and took a sip. 'An excellent cup of tea, Constable. Now, back to work.'

CHAPTER 7

As soon as he left behind the crowded streets in the centre of town, the drive to the Residence became a pleasant one. A breeze cooled his face and ruffled his hair. The road widened and was lined with more trees, although in the heat their leaves drooped.

He thought of Jane's description of spring in England. She always said it was her favourite season. After the snowdrops and aconites were over, daffodils and tulips came into flower. The trees began to put on delicate green leaves, and in the woods, great drifts of bluebells and wild garlic flowered.

The seasons didn't change as noticeably in Ceylon as they did in England. There was just the contrast between the dry months and the monsoon. Perhaps one day when he retired, they might visit England and Jane could show him an English spring. Her descriptions and those of the English poets who liked to celebrate the season made it an appealing prospect. He remembered Robert Browning's thoughts from abroad of April in England. Even though he felt sure that life in the English countryside was rarely, if ever, as idyllic as the picture Browning painted in his poem, he could understand why the idea of it occupied such a special place in English hearts.

* * *

At the Residence, fortified by his few moments of peaceful reflection on the way there, he hurried up the steps and pressed the bell. Shortly afterwards, the door was opened by a member of staff that he knew. The man smiled. 'Good afternoon, sahib. Sahib Clutterbuck is expecting you. He's in his study.'

'Thank you, I can find my own way.'

In the entrance hall, several of the staff were on their hands and knees polishing the parquet floor. Others were washing windows or running feather dusters along the joins between the ceiling and the walls. Curtains had been taken down and rugs removed. The corridor leading to the study smelled of polish. The floor gleamed, and the glass in the framed hunting prints on the walls sparkled. Florence must have given orders for a spring clean.

At the study door, de Silva paused to remove his cap. He tucked it under his arm and knocked, then hearing Archie call out, went in. Snoozing in his usual place beside his master's chair, Darcy the Labrador stirred and lumbered to his feet then ambled over to greet de Silva.

Archie put the cap on his pen and laid it down next to the pile of papers on his desk. 'Good afternoon to you de Silva,' he said with a smile. 'A hot one, eh? What brings you up here?'

This was a good start. Archie must be looking forward to his trip, whatever it was. De Silva only hoped that his news wasn't going to sour his boss's cheerful mood.

'No serious problems, I hope,' added Archie, the smile waning a little.

'I don't believe there's too much to worry about, sir, but I thought I should consult you before proceeding.'

Archie reached for a packet of cigarettes, shook one out and lit up. 'Go on.'

'It's about our illustrious guest, Dev Khan.'

'Oh?' Archie frowned. 'Has he made some kind of

complaint? I find him a very engaging fellow myself. I thought he'd been enjoying his time in Nuala.'

'I believe he has, sir, but there's been an unfortunate accident.'

As de Silva explained about the driving incident at the Crown, Archie puffed on his cigarette, his brow wrinkling.

'It's a mercy this fellow Darsh wasn't seriously hurt,' he said when de Silva had finished speaking. 'In view of the fact that Sanjeewa Gunesekera's undertaken to see to it that he's properly cared for and there are no family members to consider, coupled with Khan appearing to be prepared to admit he was driving carelessly, I think a light penalty may be in order. Before I come to a decision however, you'd better have a word with these witnesses. I'd like to hear their side of the story. Impress on them that anything they tell you is in confidence. Above all, they're to keep what they know to themselves. I don't want gossip getting out, or before you can say Jack Robinson, all kinds of wild rumours are sure to be spreading.'

'I understand, sir. The manager at the Crown is as concerned as you are to avoid publicity.'

'Good. I'm off to take part in a golf competition tomorrow and won't be here for a few days. My secretary will telephone you and let you know when I'm back. Make an appointment to report to me then and we can decide how to play this.'

'Very well, sir.'

'Do you know if Dev Khan plans to stay in Nuala for a while?'

'He and his family are booked into the Crown for another week.'

'Good, that should give us plenty of time to wrap things up. Anything else you wanted to discuss?' Archie's tone was jovial again, so de Silva decided to pose the question of the pay rises. But as he laid out his arguments to support them, the wrinkles returned to his boss's brow.

'I'll give it my consideration and let you have an answer when I'm back,' he said. 'But I can't promise anything. There's a war on, y'know. Belts are having to be tightened.'

De Silva thought that a modest increase in Prasanna and Nadar's wages seemed unlikely to jeopardise the war effort, but he kept his opinion to himself. There was no point antagonising Archie. It was usually best to give him time to get used to an idea, then he tended to be more malleable.

'Thank you, sir.'

His boss stubbed out his cigarette. 'Well, I'd better be getting on with this lot. Need to have everything cleared up before I leave in the morning.'

'I hope you have an enjoyable trip, sir.'

'I expect to. Time with old friends is always a pleasure. I only hope my game's up to the mark. There'll be some pretty stiff opposition. Still, it gets me out of Mrs Clutterbuck's hair for a few days.' His made a lugubrious face. 'I expect you noticed the spring cleaning.'

De Silva chuckled. 'I did, sir. When my wife feels the urge to begin that in our home, I spend more time than usual in the garden.'

Archie grinned. 'Very wise.'

CHAPTER 8

When he left the Residence, de Silva's original plan had been to go straight back to the station. He decided he would give Prasanna the job of interviewing the gardening staff who had witnessed the accident at the Crown. It would be good practice for him. He hadn't gone far, however, when he decided he would stop off at home first to tell Jane what had been happening. He felt reasonably confident that the situation with Dev Khan and his bad driving was going in the right direction, but it would be interesting to hear her opinion. He might even allow himself a bit of time in the garden before going back to work.

The house was quiet, and Jane was in the drawing room writing a letter. He was relieved that spring cleaning hadn't yet taken hold at Sunnybank. She looked up and smiled. 'Hello, dear. I wasn't expecting to see you home yet.'

'I've just been up to the Residence to have a word with Archie.'

'Is everything all right?'

'Yes and no.' He explained about Dev Khan's argument with his wife and the accident.

'But that's dreadful,' said Jane when he'd finished. 'How is the poor gardener?'

'Badly bruised and with a swollen ankle, but Hebden thinks he'll make a good recovery. Sanjeewa's seeing to it he's well looked after in the meantime. He'll be paid his wages while he's unable to work. He tells me he's satisfied with that.'

'It's something to be thankful for that he's being well treated, but still, he was injured, and it could have been far worse. I suppose it's not unusual for actors to be temperamental. Fame can have a detrimental effect on people's characters, but it's no excuse for such bad behaviour.'

'I entirely agree with you, but I'm not sure a heavy penalty is necessary.'

Jane thought for a few moments. 'Well,' she said at last, 'I hope that when Archie thinks it over, he doesn't decide to let him off just because he's famous, but I suppose in the circumstances a stern warning and a fine might be enough.'

'I'm glad you agree with me. And I do feel Archie's taking the matter seriously.'

'Good. It's a shame. Florence said Dev was so charming.'

'If Archie tells her, she'll probably be very disappointed to find he has feet of mud.'

'Clay, dear.'

'Ah.'

'If you can stay for a little while, shall we have some tea?'

'That would be very pleasant.'

'Will you ring the bell? I just need a few minutes to finish this letter. I want to thank Florence for lending the Residence's garden for that jumble sale to raise money for the school last week.'

As de Silva put his hand on the bellpull next to the mantelpiece, a black shadow slipped in from the hall. He bent down to stroke the little cat. She pressed her head against his hand and miaowed.

'Hello, Bella. On your own, are you?'

'Billy's probably gone hunting,' said Jane.

De Silva made a face. He was fond of Bella's brother, but he wished Billy was less keen on hunting. He knew it was an instinct in cats, but he hated to see the birds that visited the garden harmed. His Buddhist principles even made him sorry for the deaths of the mice who nibbled the young shoots in his vegetable patch. He had to admit though that he wouldn't mind so much if Billy fancied a meal of slugs and snails, but they didn't seem to hold any appeal for him.

'I'll leave you to get on with your letter. See you outside.'

With Bella following, he strolled out to the verandah. By this time of day, it was in shade, but when he leant on the rail of the balustrade to survey the garden, the wood was still warm to the touch.

Bella jumped up on one of the chairs, circled a few times then curled up in a furry, pulsating ball. He shook his head and smiled. 'We said we'd never spoil you and look what's happened.' He sat down on the other chair and heard Jane's voice and that of their servant Sria drifting from the drawing room. 'I expect your mistress will turf you off when she comes out,' he remarked to the dozing cat.

'When do you plan to talk to Archie again?' asked Jane when she emerged from the drawing room and as he had predicted, removed Bella from her chair.

'I'm not sure. I need to organise Prasanna to do the interviewing of witnesses first. I reckon it might take him the best part of a day as there were quite a few gardeners working in the area. Archie's off to play golf in some competition or other. He said his secretary would let me know when he's back. Luckily, Dev Khan is staying in Nuala for a bit longer. It would have been awkward if I'd had to arrest him to prevent him from leaving. I know British law would apply when he was back in India in the same way it does here, but it would mean involving the police in Bombay. They might not think an accident on our little island all that important. At least not in view of the greater workload that there's bound to be in the big city. The crime rate in Nuala is lower than it is in Bombay, thank goodness.'

The tea arrived and Jane poured it out. De Silva put a

spoonful of sugar in his cup and caught her looking at him pointedly.

'Only one. I haven't forgotten I promised to cut down.' He patted his middle and grinned. 'See, it's making a difference already.'

'Hmm,' said Jane sceptically then smiled. 'I'm sure it will in a few weeks' time.'

'Oh, I almost forgot, Prasanna had some news today. He and Kuveni are expecting another baby.'

'How lovely. When's it due?'

'I didn't ask.'

Jane rolled her eyes. 'Typical of a man. I must go and visit her.' She and de Silva had become very fond of Kuveni when she'd lived with them for a few months before her marriage to Prasanna.

'It came up because he and Nadar are after a rise in their pay. I've mentioned it to Archie. I realised to my shame that they've not had an increase for three years.'

'That does seem a long time. Do you think he'll agree?'

'I hope so.' He grinned. 'Especially if he wins his golf competition.'

When he'd finished a second cup of tea, de Silva wandered down to his vegetable garden. Despite all the watering that their gardener Anif did, the ground was very dry.

At that moment, Anif appeared from the direction of the fruit cage, carrying a basket of strawberries.

'Good afternoon, sahib.'

De Silva greeted him in return and looked appreciatively at the plump, scarlet fruits. 'Those look nice and ripe.'

'Yes, sahib, they will be good to eat. The memsahib told me to pick them for this evening.'

De Silva held out his hand and took the basket. He smelled the sweet fragrance of the fruit. 'I'll take them up to the house when I go.' He looked up to see where the sun was in the sky. It would be dark in an hour or so. He ought to be getting back to the station. 'About time you started the watering,' he remarked.

Anif nodded. 'I filled the butts this morning.' At this time of year, when there was almost no rain, the water butts needed to be replenished with buckets carried from the well.

'Excellent. Well, I'll leave you to it.'

With Bella exploring ahead of him, he made a quick tour of the vegetable garden to see how his plants were progressing. By the time he reached the place where rows of beans tied to cane wigwams grew, Anif had already watered them, creating dark puddles on the rich brown earth. The scarlet flowers had begun to fall, leaving little green commas behind them. He moved on to inspect a nearby bed where okra was almost ready for harvesting. Sometimes he and Jane ate it raw in a salad, but he liked it best when it was curried with tomatoes and creamed coconut.

Half hidden in the mat of leaves that the long, tapering spears rose from, Bella batted at something with her paw.

'What have you found there?'

He went over to her and saw a fat blue-black beetle flipped on its back, its myriad legs waving piteously in the air. Carefully, he placed a thumb and forefinger around the hard, shiny carapace and righted it, then keeping hold of the basket of strawberries, he scooped up Bella under his other arm. Her hind legs dangling over his hip, she looked back wistfully as they set off for the house.

CHAPTER 9

Three days passed with no call from Archie, giving Prasanna plenty of time to carry out the interviews with the gardeners who had witnessed the accident at the Crown Hotel. Nothing new had emerged from their statements. It was clear that after the argument with his wife, Dev Khan had been driving dangerously. However, fortunately for him as well as Darsh, Darsh's condition was improving rapidly. De Silva anticipated that once Archie returned, the matter would soon be settled.

It was on the following afternoon that he was at work in his office when the telephone rang. He picked up the receiver. 'There's a call for you, sir,' said Nadar.

'From the Residence?' Archie was probably back, and it was to fix up the meeting with him.

'No, sir. It's from Mr Gunesekera at the Crown. He says it's urgent.'

De Silva frowned. Urgent? He hoped there was no complication with Dev Khan.

'Put him on.'

There was a brief pause then his friend came on the line. 'Is there a problem?' asked de Silva.

'Yes, it's Dev Khan.'

'I feared you might say that. It looks as if he may get off lightly, but I'd still prefer it if he remained in Nuala until Archie's back, and we can settle matters properly. If it helps, however, I can come up and talk to him.'

He heard Sanjeewa suck air through his teeth. 'I'm afraid that won't help.'

'What do you mean?'

'He was found dead in the hotel gardens this afternoon.'

* * *

Sanjeewa met him at the hotel and led him to the place where Dev's body had been found. It was a good distance from the hotel, beyond the formal gardens: a small area of unkempt grass tucked away behind a grove of oleanders. At the back of it, an old shed with faded and blistered blue paint provided a convenient support for a heavy mass of creepers. De Silva was surprised to see Archie there. He looked up as they approached.

'Ah, de Silva, well done. Hebden and I weren't far ahead of you. I only got back a few hours ago and happened to hear the news from him. I'd told my secretary to call you in the morning about our meeting, but as you see, events have overtaken us.'

David Hebden gave de Silva a friendly nod. He indicated the body on the grass. 'Here's our man, I'm afraid. Not a happy ending.'

'And not the kind of thing Nuala wants to be in the news for,' muttered Archie.

De Silva studied Dev's lifeless form. There was no sign of the cause of death.

'I understand from his assistant, Ashok Mehta, who found him, that Khan suffered from heart problems,' said Hebden. 'And heart failure's the most likely explanation for his death.'

'He was alone when he died,' said Archie. 'There'll have to be an inquest, of course. For the family's sake as well as our own, I hope it's possible to keep the matter quiet for the moment. If that fails, there's bound to be unwelcome attention from the press.'

'Is the body as you found it?' asked de Silva.

'Yes, we've not moved it,' said Archie. 'And the area hasn't been searched. As a matter of form, I suggest you arrange that, although I doubt it will reveal anything unexpected.'

De Silva nodded. 'I'll get my men up here.'

'After he found the body, Ashok came straight up to the hotel to call for help,' said Sanjeewa. 'He was very agitated.'

'Did he have any idea what Dev was doing here? It seems a remote corner of the garden for one of the guests to be using.'

'No, he didn't. He said he'd been looking for his boss for some time.'

'I wonder if Khan had begun to feel unwell and became confused,' said Archie. 'He may have thought he was heading towards the hotel to get help but instead he was going further away from it and then he collapsed.'

'A little strange that he didn't cry out, or if he did, no one heard him. When was he found?'

'About half past three,' said Hebden. 'He was in the hotel at lunchtime so he can't have been dead for long. The other guests and most of the staff would have been taking their siestas around the time he died.'

'That would account for no one coming to his rescue,' said Archie.

De Silva didn't say anything, but he wasn't fully convinced that Archie's theory was correct. On the other hand, what other explanation could there be? If Dev had suffered heart failure in the hotel itself or in another part of the garden that was more frequented by guests or staff, surely someone would have noticed? And why would anyone move him here?

'Where's Ashok now?' he asked.

'Gone to tell Khan's wife and family the sad news,' said

Archie. 'The undertakers are on their way to collect the body. Will you wait for them here, Hebden?'

'Certainly.'

'It'll be dark soon. Do you have a torch on you?'

Hebden patted his black bag. 'Always carry one in here. You never know when it might come in handy.'

'Good. Well, I suggest the rest of us go back to the hotel and find out what's going on.'

* * *

They met Ashok as they were walking through the rose garden. 'Forgive me for not coming back sooner,' he said. 'I wasn't able to find Raj or Salman, but I've told Sunita and Layla. As one would expect, they're both extremely distressed. It would be a kindness to leave them in peace for a while if you don't mind. I've left Dev's nurse, Anne Collins, looking after them.'

He turned to de Silva. 'If you wish to talk to Raj or Salman, Inspector, I'm afraid it will have to wait, but I'll keep looking for them. If there's anyone else that you'd like to speak to, I'm at your disposal to make the necessary arrangements.'

'Good man,' intervened Archie. 'I'm sure we don't want to make your life any more difficult than it already is, do we, de Silva? Shall we go back to the hotel?'

They were shown to a quiet room in the staff quarters where they could talk in private. De Silva doubted it was used much, for it was very stuffy and there were numerous dead bluebottles on the windowsill.

'What would you like to know, Inspector?' asked Ashok.

De Silva pulled out his notebook and pencil. 'When was the last time you saw Mr Khan?'

'At lunchtime.'

'Did you have the impression he was feeling unwell?'

'He and Sunita were not on speaking terms again, and it made him irritable, but it wasn't an unusual state of affairs. His daughter Layla and I joined him for a light lunch and Sunita ate in her suite. We'd finished by half past one and I assumed he would have a siesta as he usually did.'

'What about his stepsons? Where were they?'

'I'm not sure. Salman often goes out on his own if he's not busy during the day. As for Raj, if he's not filming, I'm never too sure what he gets up to.'

Archie pulled a pack of cigarettes from his pocket. 'Mind if I smoke?'

Both men shook their heads. As Archie lit up, de Silva reflected that the smell of freshly lit tobacco was quite pleasant. It was unfortunate that it still didn't manage to mask the less agreeable odours in the stuffy room.

'You mentioned that Dev Khan was taking medicine for his heart,' said de Silva. 'Could he have missed a dose?'

'I doubt that. Anne Collins always made sure he had it.'

'Do you know what he was taking?'

'I believe it was digitoxin.'

The name wasn't familiar to de Silva. He'd have to ask Hebden about it. 'Why did you go looking for Dev when you did?'

'I realised that I'd forgotten to ask him to sign some letters. I wanted them posted today as they were quite important, so I decided to brave Dev's wrath and disturb him to give me time to put them in the afternoon post. I expected to find him in his suite, but he wasn't there.'

'Such a remote part of the garden seems a strange place for him to have gone. Can you suggest a reason why he might have been there?'

Archie looked a little impatient. 'He's already been asked that and said he doesn't know.'

'With respect, sir, I'd like to hear his answer for myself.'

'Hmm. Very well.'

'As I said to Mr Clutterbuck, I'm afraid I've no idea,' said Ashok patiently. 'I was surprised Dev even knew that part of the gardens existed. He was never much of a man for the outdoors. Even though we've been at the hotel for several weeks now, he barely set foot in the gardens.'

'Why did you look there?' asked de Silva.

For a moment Ashok seemed nonplussed then he recovered. 'After I'd found his suite empty, I'd tried all the areas close to the hotel, so I decided to work my way around the outer part of the estate. It was sheer luck I found him.'

'There you are, de Silva,' said Archie. 'Well, it looks like there's not much more we can do at the moment. Let de Silva know when the stepsons turn up will you, Mehta? When the other members of the family are past the initial shock, he can speak to them. Shall we see how Hebden's getting on, de Silva? After that I'd better get back to the Residence.' He turned to Sanjeewa. 'Thank you for your help. I expect you have work to do. Keep this under your hat, won't you?'

'Of course, sir.'

'Just as a matter of form, I suggest Dev's suite stays locked until further notice,' said de Silva. With his police-man's instincts, it was always in the back of his mind that if a search for evidence turned out to be necessary, there was a danger of it having been disturbed.

'I'll see to it,' said Sanjeewa.

When they emerged from the hotel, it was dark. They met Doctor Hebden on the drive. 'The undertakers have the body,' he said. 'I told them to leave by the back entrance.'

'Very wise,' said Archie. 'Unfortunately, the news of Khan's death will have to come out sooner or later, but one doesn't want to advertise the grim circumstances. I'll leave you and de Silva to talk. Keep me updated won't you, de Silva.'

'Yes, sir.'

'I have the impression you're not convinced by Archie's theory as to why Khan was in that part of the garden,' said David Hebden when he and de Silva were alone.

'Are you?'

'I must admit, I find the idea that he wandered into the area in a state of confusion implausible. It's at a considerable distance from the hotel.'

'And why would he want to be outdoors at all in the hottest part of the day?' asked de Silva.

'But for the moment, no explanation for his death other than heart failure springs to mind.'

'According to Ashok Mehta, he was taking a drug called digitoxin for his heart problem.'

'That's a compound of digitalis – the common foxglove. It's frequently prescribed when a patient's been diagnosed with a heart problem. In a nutshell, it regulates the transmission of the electrical signals that cause the heart to transfer oxygenated blood to the rest of the body. But it's imperative that the dose given is absolutely correct. A mistake could be fatal. Too high and the transmission of those electrical signals would be barred. The heart would be paralysed, and death would follow.'

'How long would that take?'

'If the digitoxin was given by injection, the patient would only have seconds to live, but if the overdose was taken by mouth, death might not occur for several hours.'

De Silva rubbed his chin. 'Apart from the oddness of the place where we found him, there's no reason to suppose there's been foul play, but as she was in charge of the medication, I ought to have a word with Nurse Collins anyway. I'll need her side of the story for my report.'

'By all means. Shall we find Ashok Mehta? We can ask him to arrange for someone else to sit with the wife and daughter so that Collins can come and talk with us.'

CHAPTER 10

Nurse Collins was a pretty, petite young woman. She wore a white uniform, and a few tendrils of blonde hair had escaped from under her cap. Her eyes were cornflower blue. De Silva noticed that she looked nervous.

'There's no need to be alarmed,' he said gently.

Nurse Collins gave him a tremulous smile. 'It's about Dev Khan that you want to see me, isn't it? I'll be glad to help in any way I can.'

'I understand he had a weak heart.'

'Yes. He'd been prescribed digitoxin by his doctor. I gave it to him each day.'

'Can you confirm you did so yesterday?'

'Of course.' Anne Collins flushed. 'I've been in charge of giving him his medication for a long time. I hope you're not suggesting I made an error.'

'At the moment, we're suggesting nothing,' said de Silva calmly. 'But as he was alone when he died, I have to ask certain questions. I have to be satisfied that there are no suspicious circumstance surrounding his death, and of course, as no medical practitioner was present, there'll have to be an autopsy and an inquest.'

'An autopsy?'

De Silva thought he heard a note of alarm in her voice, but she swiftly rallied. 'I assure you I always took the greatest care over Dev's medication. I know how important it is to give a patient the correct amount and at the same time each day.'

'What time was that?'

'Shortly after breakfast.'

'Did you give it by injection or by mouth?'

'I don't understand why you need to know that, but it was by mouth. Dev hated injections.'

'Did you notice anything different about him today? Anything that concerned you?'

'I'm afraid I didn't,' she said with a sigh. 'If I had done, I would have tried to persuade him to rest. Particularly as he'd been working so hard.'

'What about the making up of the prescription?' asked Hebden.

'It was dispensed by our regular clinic in Bombay, and I brought it with us. I've been using the batch for several weeks. I'm sure there can't have been anything wrong with it.'

That did seem convincing, thought de Silva. The thing that still troubled him, however, was what Dev had been doing in that remote part of the garden when he died. If there'd been any wounds on the body, he might have thought someone had lured him there to take revenge for the injury to Darsh, but that wasn't the case.

He thought of Ashok's claim that it was pure luck that had led him to find his boss. The conversation he'd overheard between the young man and Layla up at the cricket club came back to him. Some might say it was coincidence, but he'd sometimes wondered whether there was such a thing as coincidence where crime was concerned. Were there just moments when an underlying pattern could be seen in the fabric of events? Had Dev Khan died of unnatural causes after all?

Maybe Ashok had found a way of getting hold of some of his boss's medication. If that was the case, was Layla in on the plan? Apparently, Dev had doted on her but her love for Ashok might have become a stronger force in her life. Would she have helped him to do away with her father, or at least kept silent and let him carry out the crime? It was a shocking thought, but he had to consider it.

David Hebden's voice interrupted his thoughts.

'I don't think we need to detain Nurse Collins any longer, do you?'

'No, I think that will be all for now. Thank you, you've been most helpful. If there are any other questions, I'll be in touch.'

* * *

'That all seems satisfactory,' said Hebden as they walked to their cars. 'If she accidentally gave him the wrong dose at breakfast time, and we've no reason to distrust her word that it was the correct dose, he would have collapsed before lunchtime, irrespective of whether the dose was given orally or by injection.'

De Silva didn't reply.

'There's something bothering you,' said Hebden. 'I know that look.'

'I may have been imagining it, but did you think she looked alarmed when I mentioned an autopsy?'

'I can't say I noticed. Mind you, some people find the idea unpleasant, particularly where someone they knew well is involved.'

'But she's a nurse. Shouldn't she be used to medical procedures?'

Hebden shrugged. 'It may be a long time since she's dealt with anything much apart from administering Dev's Khan's medication or seeing to minor injuries and everyday ailments. Anyway, as I said, the timing indicates she didn't make a mistake.'

'But just as a matter of interest, let's suppose that later someone gave Dev an overdose.'

'Then it would be much harder to get at the truth. An overdose of digitoxin needs to be a large one to show up in an autopsy. In fact far larger than would be necessary to kill a man. I believe that's why over the years the drug has been popular with people wanting to dispose of burdensome friends or relations.' He frowned. 'But why are you asking? Are you suggesting that someone did deliberately give him an overdose?'

De Silva decided not to go into detail just yet. He wanted time to think. 'No, no,' he said quickly. 'I'm just interested in the subject.'

'Well, here we are.' Hebden lifted the boot of his car and stowed his black bag inside. 'I'd better be off. Emerald will be wondering where I've got to. I'll organise the autopsy in the morning and let you have the report as soon as possible.'

'Thank you.'

CHAPTER 11

As he drove to the station, de Silva once more went over the meeting with Anne Collins in his head. Had he imagined that she'd looked nervous at the mention of an autopsy, and if she had been, was David Hebden right about why? It was dark now, so the search of the area where Dev had been found would have to wait until the morning. He'd send Nadar as well as Prasanna. He'd impress on them that they must be very thorough.

When he passed the bazaar, he saw that most of the stallholders had already packed up. In the dim light cast by a few oil lamps, a troop of monkeys lolloped down one of the lanes, no doubt on the hunt for discarded fruit and vegetables. When he stopped at a corner to let a man with a handcart cross in front of the Morris, a dog lapping up the contents of a broken egg lying in the gutter half raised its head and bared its teeth. Its bloodshot eyes gleamed like miniature fires. The sight reminded him that in life, violence was never far beneath the surface.

Prasanna and Nadar were both in the public room when he came in.

'We didn't like to lock up until you came back, sir,' said Prasanna.

De Silva wondered how much this conscientiousness owed to their hope of a pay rise. They didn't usually stay so late. He was sorry he had nothing encouraging to tell them.

'What's the news from the hotel, sir?' asked Nadar.

'Doctor Hebden thinks Mr Khan died of heart failure.'

'Are you not sure about that, sir?' asked Prasanna.

De Silva smiled. 'Very perceptive of you, Sergeant. Despite the respect I have for Doctor Hebden's opinions, let's say I'd like to reserve judgment for now. I've reason to believe that Khan's assistant, Ashok Mehta, would have liked him out of the way. Ashok and Khan's daughter have feelings for each other, and it was likely Khan would have been against their getting married. Also, when Doctor Hebden and I spoke to Khan's nurse, her nervous demeanour perturbed me. But you're to keep all of this to yourselves for the moment.'

The two young men nodded.

'Tomorrow I'd like the two of you to cycle over to the Crown Hotel. Mr Khan's body was found in the gardens, and I want you to make a thorough search of the area. I don't want it to be obvious that you're policemen so wear your own clothes. I'll arrange with Mr Gunesekera for him to meet you somewhere away from the hotel and show you where to search.' De Silva paused. It might be difficult to keep his friend Sanjeewa in the dark. He'd have to decide what to do about that.

'What are we looking for, sir?' asked Nadar.

'Anything you wouldn't expect to find in a garden,' said de Silva briskly.

* * *

'I've just come in myself,' said Jane when he arrived at Sunnybank and found her in the hall taking off her hat. 'I went to visit Emerald this afternoon and stayed longer than I planned. What sad news about Dev Khan. David came home just as I was leaving and told us about it.'

'Yes, it is sad news. I'm not sure if all of the family know yet. When I left the Crown, Ashok Mehta had told Dev's wife and his daughter, Layla, but he hadn't managed to find his stepsons.'

He picked up Bella who was rubbing up against his leg in greeting. There was no sign of Billy. *Probably out hunting again*, de Silva thought ruefully.

'I imagine the ladies were very distressed,' said Jane. 'I hope Dev and his wife were on good terms before it happened. I'm sure it would make a sad situation worse if their last words were spoken in anger.'

'I'm afraid that might have been the case. Ashok told me that he and Layla had lunch with Dev, but Sunita ate alone in her suite because they'd quarrelled again.'

Still carrying Bella, he followed Jane into the drawing room and sat down. Jane went to the garden door and opened it to let in the evening air then came to join him. She sighed. 'Oh dear, it's probably something she'll regret for a long time. I wonder what will happen about the film. It may never be finished now.'

'I imagine that will depend on who inherits the company. Sanjeewa mentioned that Dev and his stepsons didn't always get on well, but he doted on his daughter, and as they say, blood is thicker than water. If she inherits, I doubt it would be easy for her to run the show on her own, especially as she's still very young, but she may be able to rely on Ashok for help. I believe they're in love.'

'Why do you say that?'

'Because I overheard them talking in private when I went to the film set to see how the packing up of all the equipment was going. I didn't mean to intrude, and I had the definite impression my presence was unwelcome. I'm sure they wanted to keep their relationship quiet.'

'Did you hear what they were saying?'

He hesitated. He had so little in the way of proof, but he knew Jane would be discreet.

'Shanti?'

'I'm only telling you, Prasanna, and Nadar this, but I'm not convinced that David's view that Dev died of heart failure is correct. First of all, his body was found in a very out-of-the-way part of the garden. There was no obvious reason why he should have been there.'

'That does sound rather strange.'

'It was Ashok who found him. And in the conversation that I overheard between him and Layla, he said something about if they did nothing, he – by that I think he could have meant Dev – would never allow them to be free.'

'But to kill him! Gracious, Shanti, do you really believe Layla would agree to murdering her own father? Surely, her conscience would torment her unbearably, however much she loves Ashok.'

'Even so, I can't ignore it. Alternatively, it may have been what Ashok had in mind even if she didn't. She may have thought Ashok simply meant they must run away together.'

'Are you convinced that Dev would have opposed a match between them? After all, he came from a modest background himself.'

'Ashok certainly seemed to think there was no hope. Perhaps he knew Dev had grander plans for his daughter.'

'But Dev's death changes everything,' mused Jane.

'Yes.'

'What about the rest of the family? Might this be about money and power rather than love? They might hope to inherit Dev's money and be rid of him because he was too overbearing. Then they could run the film business as they wanted.'

'Maybe, although I have nothing to link them to the death at the moment.'

'But something might turn up.'

'It might. According to Sanjeewa, Salman seems withdrawn and unhappy, and not very interested in the filming work, but that might change with Dev no longer around. Since Raj is an actor, one would expect him to be more interested in continuing with the business, and the same goes for Sunita, although if she's as temperamental as she's reputed to be, she might not have the cool head needed.'

'That wouldn't necessarily stop her from trying.'

'True.' He paused for a moment before he spoke again. The gauzy cream curtains at the garden door stirred gently in the breeze. 'I also thought there was something odd about the way the nurse in charge of Dev's medication reacted when we mentioned that an autopsy would have to be carried out. David thought she was just upset at the thought of it, but I'm not entirely convinced.'

'Could she have given Dev an overdose?'

'Not when she gave him his regular medication that morning, but I suppose it's possible she did so later.'

'Goodness, so many people to consider. Where will you start?'

'I'm sending Prasanna and Nadar up to the Crown tomorrow to make a thorough search of the area where Dev was found.' He looked at his watch. 'That reminds me, I must telephone Sanjeewa and make the arrangement with him. I don't want Prasanna and Nadar raising any suspicion that the police are investigating the death. Do I have time before dinner?'

Jane nodded. 'It won't be ready for half an hour.'

'Then I'll try and catch him now.' He put Bella on the floor, and she gave a little miaow of protest.

'Good idea.'

'All done,' he said when he returned to the drawing room. 'He's going to meet them near the tennis courts and if anyone asks, he'll say they've come to look at doing some maintenance work there. I've already told them to wear plain clothes. Thankfully, he was too busy to ask questions about what's going on. I haven't decided what to do about involving him yet.'

He went to the sideboard and poured himself a whisky and soda and a sherry for Jane then sat down again in his chair. Bella jumped back onto his lap and proceed to wash one of her front paws. 'When the time's right to speak to Layla about Dev's death, it will be interesting to see how she reacts. Unfortunately, if Ashok found a way of giving Dev an overdose of his medication to make it look as if he died of heart failure, it's likely to be very hard to prove. David told me that detecting an overdose of the drug is very difficult. It needs to be far larger than would be needed to kill the victim. If the murderer knew anything about the poison, they'd be unlikely to make that mistake.'

'True.' Jane frowned. 'But there's something in the back of my mind. A true crime I once read about where a small but fatal overdose was detected. I think, however, in that case the victim vomited before they died and there were traces of the poison detected in the vomit.'

'Maybe it's unfortunate that Dev was spared that indignity.'

'Oh yes, and I recall reading about another crime. It involved a Frenchwoman who took a lover and then poisoned her husband. She received a substantial payment from an insurance policy on her husband's life, and she and the lover enjoyed spending it, until she tired of him too and poisoned him. After that she lived an extravagant life in fashionable society, apparently poisoning several friends for their money as well. When she ran out of friends, she began to poison her customers. She'd offer them cups of tea laced with digitalis when they came for fittings and then take any money and valuables that they had with them. Rumours began to circulate about her but what proved to be her undoing was an incident where a woman friend had been complaining to her about her husband. She offered the friend a powder that would dispatch him and leave no trace. The woman decided to go to the police.'

'I'm glad to hear it.'

'The murderess was arrested, the bodies of many of her victims were exhumed, and traces of digitalis were found, but I suppose that means she must have given them large overdoses. She was found guilty of ten murders although there may have been many more.'

'A case to strike terror into the hearts of husbands everywhere.'

Jane laughed. 'I don't think you need worry.'

'But I'll certainly look on the cups of tea you offer me in a new light,' said de Silva with a grin.

CHAPTER 12

Hart's Pharmaceutical Chemist was on the same street as Bentleys, the department store where most of the British ladies liked to do their shopping. On either side of the glass door there were large windows set in intricate mahogany frames. Above, the shop's name was spelled out in elaborate gold lettering.

Inside the shop, a plethora of small mahogany drawers, all neatly labelled with mysteriously named contents, lined the lower half of each side wall. Above them, porcelain jars with descriptions of their contents painted in flamboyant lettering stood on shelves along with tall, swan-necked glass bottles that might have come from the *Tales of the Arabian Nights*. As she crossed the threshold the following morning to the accompaniment of the jangling bell attached to the door, Jane smelled the familiar aromas of beeswax, soap, and antiseptic.

Dressed in white overalls and with his bald head gleaming like a billiard ball, Mr Hart was behind the counter making up a prescription for a lady customer. A few moments passed before Jane noticed that Florence Clutterbuck was also in the shop. She smiled when she saw Jane and they wished each other good morning.

'I hope no one in your household is unwell,' said Florence.

'Oh no, I've just come in to buy some Reckitt's Blue.

We've run out and I want Delisha to use it to whiten the sheets next time she launders them. It's been so hot in the last few days that I thought I'd do my shopping early.'

Florence glanced at the customer being served by the pharmacist. 'I hope she won't take too much longer,' she muttered. 'I want to ask Mr Hart if he has any other reading spectacles in stock.' She held up the pair in her hand. 'If needs be, I'll have to buy these for now, but I'd rather have more to choose from.'

Jane knew that Florence had worn spectacles for reading and close work for several years. 'Have you lost your usual pair?' she asked.

Florence frowned. 'It's very curious. I can't think what's happened to them. I was sitting on the terrace reading one afternoon – of course I rarely have time for such pursuits during the day, but the book was one that needed to go back to the library.'

Jane smiled. She suspected that with all the servants employed at the Residence, if she wanted it, Florence quite often had time to herself in the day, although to be fair she was assiduous about organising many local activities.

'One of the servants came out to tell me that Archie was looking for me. I went inside for a few minutes to see what he wanted and when I came back, my book was still lying open as I'd left it, but my reading spectacles which I'd left on top of it were missing. I wondered if they'd somehow fallen on the floor, so I called one of the servants who searched for me. She couldn't find them either.'

'Could you have been mistaken and taken them inside with you? Maybe you had them in your hand and didn't put them down on the book after all.'

Florence gave her a stern look. 'I'm sure I left them outside. I'll be sorry if they're lost for good. They were a particularly nice pair. The frames were tortoiseshell with a gold trim.'

'I remember them.'

Florence glanced back to the counter where the lady was deep in conversation with the pharmacist. 'I shall have to go in a few moments,' she said in a slightly louder voice than was necessary. 'I've an important meeting back at the Residence.'

The lady at the counter turned and looked flustered. 'Mrs Clutterbuck! I didn't see you there. Forgive me if I'm holding you up.' Quickly, she took the parcel that the pharmacist had wrapped up. 'Put it on my account, please.'

'Yes, madam.'

The bell jangled as the shop door closed behind her.

'I'm sorry you were kept waiting, Mrs Clutterbuck,' said Mr Hart. 'What can I do for you today?'

'Do you have any other spectacles in stock?' Florence held up the pair that failed to please.

'I'm afraid not, madam. I can order some from Colombo, but it will take a week or so.'

'I can't wait that long. These will have to do. I'll take them.'

The spectacles wrapped and charged to her account, Florence handed the parcel to a servant who seemed to have materialised out of thin air and told him to summon the official car to the front of the shop. She said goodbye to Jane and the pharmacist hurried to hold the door open for her.

When he came back, Jane asked for her Reckitt's Blue. Whilst she waited for him to fetch it from the stockroom, she thought about Florence's story. It was strange that the spectacles had vanished without an explanation. In her experience, Florence wasn't usually absentminded.

* * *

De Silva arrived at the police station to find Prasanna and Nadar dressed in plain clothes and waiting to set off. After he gave them their instructions and reminded them to be thorough, they cycled away. Left alone, he looked around the public room; it was very tidy. He smiled to himself. The hope of a pay rise was paying dividends. He only hoped that Archie would come through with it. Unfortunately now was probably not the best time to raise the matter again.

At intervals as he got on with his work, he wondered whether he should have gone to the Crown himself, but he was far more likely to be recognised than his junior officers. Anyway, he ought to trust them to do a thorough job as he'd instructed.

It was nearly midday when he heard voices in the public room then a brisk knock on the door.

'Come in,' he called.

The door opened and Prasanna appeared followed by Nadar.

'I was beginning to wonder where the two of you'd got to.'

'You said we needed to be thorough, sir,' said Prasanna. De Silva noticed that both he and Nadar were looking very pleased with themselves. Had they found something?

'Well, don't keep me in suspense.'

'We could see where the body had been because the grass was all flattened, so we searched there first, but we didn't find anything. After that, I took half of the rest of the clearing and Nadar took the other half. We got down on our hands and knees and went over those areas as thoroughly as we could. The door to the old shed wasn't locked so we tried in there too, but all we found were spiders and dust and a few broken gardening tools and bits of equipment.'

'We were wondering whether we ought to widen the search,' chipped in Nadar, 'but before we did, I pulled a loose plank off the shed and used it to beat down that weedy patch in front of it. That was when we saw something glint. It must have been thrown under the floor of the shed, but we managed to pull it out.'

Prasanna held out a small see-through bag.

As he raised it to the light and studied its contents, de Silva felt his stomach give a little flip of excitement; he'd been right to be suspicious. The bag contained a syringe. It was not something one expected to find in a patch of weeds, and even more interestingly, there was a faint residue of whiteish liquid inside it. De Silva opened the mouth of the bag carefully and gave it a sniff but there was no odour. He closed the bag again.

'I hope you wore gloves before it went in the bag,' he said.

'I did, sir,' Prasanna said proudly.

'Good. The syringe will need to be checked for fingerprints. Deal with that please.'

'Yes, sir,' said Prasanna.

'And make a note of the exact time and place at which it was found.'

'We already have.'

De Silva smiled. 'A good job done, both of you. If the residue in the syringe is shown to be digitoxin, the drug Dev Khan was taking for his weak heart, I think we have our proof that he didn't die of natural causes. Considering that you found the syringe tucked under the shed behind those weeds, it seems unlikely that he put it there himself. Anyway, there were no scratch marks on his hands. In addition, the nurse who's in charge of giving him the medicine told me that he had a horror of needles. No, if he wanted to do away with himself, he would have been more likely to swallow an overdose than inject it.'

'And he wouldn't have needed to hide himself away in the garden to do that,' said Prasanna.

'That's right. Now, I want you to keep your discovery

to yourselves. The official line is still that Dev Khan died of heart failure, and I want that to be what people believe happened until we have a clearer picture of what's been going on.'

'Do you think the newspapers will be interested, sir?' asked Nadar, his eyes widening.

'I do, and Mr Clutterbuck is already concerned about Nuala's name being associated with a scandal. It would be extremely unfortunate if that were to happen, and I'm sure he'd be very displeased. Above all, if Khan was murdered, we don't want the killer to suspect we might be onto them.'

He reached for the telephone. 'I'll give Doctor Hebden a call. I'd like him to see this syringe. Hopefully, he'll be able to find out for us what's in it. If it's digitoxin, Nurse Collins has questions to answer about how someone managed to get hold of it.'

CHAPTER 13

'Doctor Hebden's been called out to see a seriously ill patient,' said his receptionist. 'Their plantation's rather remote, so we're not expecting him back for some time.'

The patient at the remote plantation would be seriously ill today of all days, de Silva thought irritably.

'But not to worry,' the receptionist went on in a bright tone. 'If it's about the late Mr Khan, the pathologist is doing the autopsy today. The doctor will let you know the result as soon as he has the report. Would you like him to telephone you in any event when he comes back?'

'Yes, please.'

'I'll make sure he knows.'

De Silva thanked her and went to see how Prasanna and Nadar were getting on with the fingerprinting.

* * *

'Sorry to have kept you waiting, old chap,' said Hebden when he called.

'No apology is necessary. I know you're a man much in demand.'

Hebden laughed ruefully. 'One shouldn't complain. I just wish some of my patients didn't live in such out-of-the-way places. Anyway, I heard that my receptionist informed you the autopsy is in hand. I should have the report soon.'

'She did, but it wasn't that I was ringing about. There's been an interesting development. I sent my officers up to make a search of the place where Dev Khan's body was found, and they came back with something.' He explained about the syringe. 'My officers have checked it and there are no fingerprints, but it looks as if it's been used recently. There's a residue of liquid in the tube.'

'Do you want to bring it over here now and I'll take a look? I have time to spare. My receptionist wasn't sure what time I'd be back, so she cancelled some of my afternoon appointments.'

'Thank you. I'll be with you shortly.'

* * *

De Silva didn't often visit Hebden's surgery. It was housed in a two-storey Victorian building that had once been a branch of a bank. The cavernous waiting room where the counters would have been now contained only a reception desk and a few chairs for the use of patients waiting to see the doctor. A square of red carpet covered the centre of the wood-block floor. Various framed certificates testifying to Hebden's qualifications hung over an incongruously splendid mahogany mantelpiece, on which stood a plaster bust of Britannia. In one corner of the room, a flight of stairs zigzagged up into the shadows.

The receptionist greeted him with a smile. 'Doctor Hebden's waiting for you, Inspector de Silva. I'll let him know you're here.'

'Thank you.'

'So, we assume this was used to attack Khan. Is that it?' asked Hebden when they'd settled down in his consulting room and de Silva had produced the bag containing the syringe.

'I'd say there's a distinct chance of that.'

Hebden nodded. 'It seems the most plausible explanation for what it would be doing in a patch of weeds near to where we found the body.'

'It's a pity there are no fingerprints. My officers checked and found none. That would have made my task a lot easier but, if possible, I'd like to know what the substance in the syringe is.'

'If you have no objection, I'll remove it from the bag.'

'Please do.'

When he'd taken a closer look, Hebden put the syringe into the bag again and handed it back. 'I can't say for sure and there's not much in there, but the laboratory chaps should be able to identify what it is for us. If it is digitoxin, it's much easier to identify when it's not inside a body.'

'Good. Whilst we wait for the results, I intend to speak to Nurse Collins again.'

'Are you suggesting that she was involved?'

'It's something that has to be considered. But if she is innocent, she still has questions to answer. She was in charge of the medicine, so if someone else got hold of it, I'd like to know how and who they were. In any case, the medicine bottle ought to be checked for fingerprints.'

'If it will help, I'll come with you.'

'Thank you.'

* * *

De Silva stopped off at the station to telephone ahead and change into the civilian clothes he kept in his office. He decided it might be a good idea if he didn't keep turning up at the Crown in uniform and drawing attention to himself. When he and Hebden arrived, Sanjeewa had arranged for Nurse Collins to meet them in the small lounge off the lobby where de Silva had interviewed Dev Khan after the car accident. They'd decided that they wouldn't try to hide the reason for their visit from her.

'I'm not sure I can add anything to what I've already told you,' she said when they'd sat down. Instead of her nurse's uniform, she wore a full-skirted, sky-blue summer frock. Her blonde curls were immaculate, and she was more heavily made up than she'd been on the previous occasion that they'd spoken to her. 'But of course I'm willing to help in any way I can.'

'Thank you,' said de Silva. 'I'm afraid that what we have to tell you may come as a shock. We have reason to believe that Dev Khan was murdered.'

'Murdered! But that's impossible. It was heart failure. You said so yourself, Doctor Hebden.'

'And at the time, I believed it but something new has come to light. A used syringe was found near the body. It's been sent to the laboratory for analysis, but I expect them to confirm that the substance remaining in it is digitoxin, the medicine Dev was taking for his heart. You mentioned that he had a horror of needles, so we assume that he wasn't the one to use it. As I'm sure you're aware, digitoxin is a powerful drug. Even a small overdose can kill.'

Anne Collins had turned pale. 'But why would anyone want to harm him?' She hesitated. 'I hope you're not suggesting—'

'No one's accusing you of anything,' said de Silva. 'But we'd like to know what precautions you've been taking to keep the digitoxin safe.'

'Why, I've kept it here at the Crown, in my room. Along with all my medical equipment.'

'Apart from the hotel staff, can you think of anyone who might be able to enter your room without your knowledge?'

'I don't know… I mean I don't think so.'

'But even if they were able to,' persisted de Silva, 'is

the medicine locked away?' He looked at her closely, but she wouldn't meet his eye. For a few moments she seemed distracted.

'Nurse Collins,' he prompted. 'I'd like an answer, please. If someone entered your room without permission, could they have found the digitoxin?'

She flushed. 'I didn't keep it locked up. I never thought there was any need to.'

'And do you have any reason to suppose someone did get into your room?'

There was a long pause. 'There was a time when it might have happened,' she said awkwardly. 'I was about to go down to dinner one evening when the lights went out in my room. I didn't have a torch with me or anything, so I found my way to the door thinking they'd be on in the corridor, but they weren't. I was wondering what to do when I saw a light. There was a man at the far end of the corridor, and he was carrying a torch.'

'Did you recognise him?'

She shook her head, her words coming more rapidly now. 'He wasn't a guest. He told me he was one of the hotel's maintenance men. There'd been a report of a problem with the electricity on my floor and he'd been sent up to see what the matter was. I thought it was a bit strange that my lights had only just gone off and there'd been a report already, but he said the report had been made quite a while ago. Presumably it had only affected some rooms. He said was sorry if I'd had a fright. He'd thought all the guests on the corridor had already gone for dinner – I was rather late – so it would be alright to turn the electricity supply off. He needed to do that to fix the problem.'

'What happened then?'

'He said it would be safer not to turn the electricity back on yet. He needed to do a bit more work first. He asked me to leave my door open so he could check my room.'

'And did you agree?'

'Yes, then he walked me to the end of the corridor and through the door into the lobby where the lights were on.'

'Is the lock on the door to your room of the self-locking Yale type?'

Anne Collins looked flustered as she shook her head.

'Did you ask what this electrician was going to do about locking it when he'd finished his work?'

'I forgot to,' she said awkwardly. 'I suppose I must have thought he would have a staff pass key.'

'So if he'd wanted to, he had plenty of time to search your room.'

'Yes,' she answered in a small voice.

'Describe this man for me.'

'He was a little shorter than you. Heavily built. I'm sorry, that's all I can tell you. With the torch beam shining at me, it was hard to see his face.'

'I think we'd better have a look at the bottle of digitoxin, don't you,' said Hebden. 'Would you show us the way to your room, please, Nurse Collins?'

The room was a modest one, but it was pleasantly decorated with cream paint on the walls and curtains patterned with pink roses. The bedspread was made of pink candlewick fabric. There was a mahogany cupboard and chest of drawers as well as a small dressing table. Its surface displayed a considerable number of pots of makeup, brushes, and a bottle of Yardley's "Red Roses" perfume. A light floral fragrance perfumed the air.

Nurse Collins went to the chest of drawers and opened the top one. She reached in and brought out a small brown bottle. 'Here it is.'

She held it out to de Silva who pulled a handkerchief from his pocket and took it carefully by its neck.

'I'll need to check it for fingerprints and take yours too so they can be eliminated. That will involve your accompanying me to the station.'

'After the evening that you saw this maintenance man, did you notice anything unusual about the amount remaining in the bottle?' asked Hebden.

'I don't understand.' There was something evasive in her tone.

'I mean was it emptier than you would expect?'

'I... I can't be sure.'

'The amount remaining is easily measured,' he said sternly. 'How many doses had you given Mr Khan up until the morning of his death?'

'I don't recall.' Nurse Collins flushed again. There was a sheen of moisture on her forehead. 'I can't say for sure when I started with this particular bottle.'

'Do you keep any syringes?' asked de Silva.

'Well, yes. Of course I didn't need any to give Dev his medication, but I might need one for other things.'

'Is one missing?'

A faint look of defiance flitted across her face. 'I'm not sure exactly how many I had with me.'

'I see,' said Hebden dryly.

There was a moment of silence before her eyes filled with tears. 'I haven't done anything. You can't believe I killed him.' She began to shake.

'Calm yourself,' said Hebden.

'I... I'm sorry.' She gripped the edge of the open drawer. 'Are you going to arrest me?'

'No,' said de Silva. 'But until we've got to the bottom of this, for your own safety, I'll ask the manager to find you another room for a few days. Your meals can be served to you there.'

'Thank you.' The words were uttered in a whisper.

'One last thing,' de Silva went on. 'Where were you on the afternoon that Mr Khan died?'

'I was at the swimming pool. I wasn't needed that afternoon, so I decided to go there and relax. I didn't come back up to my room until teatime.'

'Were you alone?'

'Yes, but there were pool attendants there and other guests, not that I'm acquainted with any of them.'

'Thank you. I have someone else to see but please wait for me here. I'll collect you shortly and take you to the police station.'

* * *

'What do you make of that?' asked Hebden as they returned to the lobby.

'If she was making up the story as she went along, she has a fertile imagination. On the other hand if it's true, the part about the locking up shows a lamentable lack of care for security. I'd like a word with Sanjeewa. If this maintenance man existed, there should be a record of a problem in the maintenance department's incident book. I noticed there was no telephone in her room, so Collins won't be able to contact anyone without leaving it. I'll ask Sanjeewa to do what he can to keep an eye on her movements.'

'Do you really think she's involved?'

'I'm not sure. It should be a simple enough matter to confirm her alibi, but that doesn't mean to say she wasn't helping the murderer. She might have given them a syringe and enough digitoxin to kill Dev. The story about the power cut may be a lie.'

They'd reached the lobby. Hebden looked up at the clock above the reception desk. 'I'd better be getting back to the surgery. I'm sorry to leave you with the problem. I'll be interested to know what you find out.'

As he walked away, de Silva's thoughts turned to his friend Sanjeewa. As all of the suspects were staying at the hotel, if he was going to investigate the case with any degree of secrecy, he'd need Sanjeewa's help. It wouldn't be the first occasion on which he'd turned to him, but de Silva anticipated that this time it would be to a far greater extent than before. It was one thing involving David Hebden, Archie was well-acquainted with him and trusted him. Hebden was also bound by his professional code of conduct. Where Sanjeewa was concerned, however, although de Silva had no doubts about his trustworthiness, it was probably wise to clear the ground with Archie first. He might already have gone further than he should without doing so.

The public telephone booth in the lobby was unoccupied. He hurried over to it and placed a call to the Residence. When it was answered, he asked to speak to Archie.

After a few moments, the message came back that Archie wasn't available but would see him in the morning.

'Please ask him again,' said de Silva. 'I'll try not to take up too much of his time, but it's important I talk to him without delay.'

'Very well, Inspector.'

Eventually, Archie came on the line. 'What's this all about, de Silva? It had better be as urgent as you say it is. We have important guests here.'

'It's about Dev Khan.'

'What about him?'

'Evidence has come to light that he was murdered.'

'Good God, man!'

De Silva winced and held the telephone receiver away from his ear.

'Are you sure about this?'

'I'm afraid so.' He explained about the digitoxin.

'What about suspects?' asked Archie. 'No, you'd better keep that for tomorrow. I must get back to our visitors. Is there anything that can't wait?'

'All the current suspects are residents at the hotel. It will be much easier to make discreet enquiries with the help of the manager, Sanjeewa Gunesekera.'

'Hmm, take him into our confidence, you mean. It's irregular.'

'I appreciate that, sir, but I believe he can be relied upon to observe the need for secrecy. I've known him a long time and he's used to protecting the privacy of his guests.'

A growly, rumbling sound came from the other end of the line. De Silva knew that it meant Archie was thinking.

'Very well,' his boss said eventually. 'Do as you think best, but remember, if it goes wrong, both our jobs could be on the line. We'll speak in the morning. I'll get my secretary to telephone you as soon as our guests have left.'

De Silva hung up and went over to the front desk. 'I'd like to see Mr Gunesekera,' he said to one of the receptionists.

'Certainly, Inspector. I'll let him know.'

CHAPTER 14

In the staff area of the hotel, de Silva was asked to wait outside his friend's office.

'I'm sorry to keep you waiting, sahib,' said the man who'd shown him the way. 'Mr Gunesekera is dealing with a problem with one of the staff. He'll try not to keep you too long.'

'There's no need to apologise. He wasn't expecting me.'

After two or three minutes, a young woman dressed in chambermaid's uniform emerged, wiping her eyes. As she scuttled past him, de Silva put his head around the door. Sanjeewa smiled wearily. 'Hello, Shanti. To what do I owe the pleasure?'

'I'm sorry, I've obviously come at a bad time. Can you spare a few moments? I just need some information.'

'Of course, come in. It was only a bit of trouble with one of our guests. A harpy called Mrs Patel. She claims that Mara, the chambermaid who was just in here, broke a very expensive bottle of perfume that was almost full.'

'And what does your chambermaid say?'

'She admits she broke it but says it was nearly empty. Mrs Patel came into the bedroom in her suite and shouted at her – something about the cushions on the chaise longue in the drawing room not being arranged the way she wanted them. She startled Mara who turned around too fast. The bottle was on the edge of the dressing table.

She accidentally swept it off and it shattered on the floor.'

'Who do you believe?'

'Mara. She's been with us for years and she's always done an excellent job. The Patel woman's been trouble ever since the day she arrived. That was already a difficult one and she made it much worse.'

'Oh?'

'You know, it was the day when Dev ran our gardener down.'

'Ah yes, I remember a large lady making a nuisance of herself in the lobby. Was that her?'

Sanjeewa rolled his eyes. 'Yes, that was her. One gets difficult guests from time to time, but she's in a class of her own. As the saying goes, some guests give us pleasure when they arrive and others when they leave.' He shrugged. 'At least her husband is less objectionable.'

'I hope the trouble soon blows over,' said de Silva, painfully aware he was about to bring something much worse down on Sanjeewa's head.

'Oh, I expect it will, and I'm glad to say that the Patels won't be staying much longer. In the meantime, she has to be pacified. I've already had flowers and champagne delivered to her suite, and I've offered a complimentary dinner as well as an adjustment to the bill to cover the perfume. The price she claims she paid for it seems to me to be extortionately expensive. Still, I don't want bad publicity for the hotel. Now, enough of the Patels. What can I do for you?'

When de Silva asked him about the power cut, Sanjeewa's brow furrowed.

'I'm surprised I've heard nothing about it. I like to keep abreast of everything that goes on in the hotel and the staff know that. I'll have a word with the maintenance department.'

He picked up the telephone. A few moments passed before the call was answered. He spoke briefly to the person at the other end of the line then finished the call. 'They'll check and get back to me as soon as possible. Can you wait here for a while?'

'Not a problem.'

'What's all this about anyway?' Sanjeewa gave him a shrewd look. 'If it has to do with the hotel, I want to know. I assure you, whatever it is will go no further unless you authorise me to tell anyone.'

'I can't stress too strongly how important that is. Archie Clutterbuck's agreed to my taking you into my confidence, but I hope you won't be offended that his agreement was conditional on absolute secrecy.'

'I wouldn't expect anything else.'

'Thank you. I'm afraid there's reason to believe that Dev Khan didn't die from natural causes.'

Briefly, Sanjeewa looked bewildered then he put his head in his hands. When he raised it again, his expression was haggard. 'Mrs Patel and her tantrums are rapidly paling into insignificance. You think he was murdered in my hotel? Shanti my old friend, what hornets' nest have you stirred up? Are you sure about this?'

'I had my men search the area of the garden where Dev's body was found. They found a used syringe.'

Sanjeewa rubbed a hand over his chin and frowned. 'So, are you thinking it was used on Dev Khan?'

'Yes, probably to give him an overdose of the heart medicine he was taking. David Hebden tells me that when given by injection, an overdose will cause death almost immediately. If he was attacked, he wouldn't have had time to get help.'

'Are you sure someone else was involved?'

'You mean suicide? I think that can be ruled out.'

'Does anyone apart from you, Mr Clutterbuck, and Doctor Hebden know about this?'

'Hebden and I spoke to Nurse Collins. She's admitted

the medicine wasn't kept locked up. It was just in a drawer.'

He recounted her story about the maintenance man. 'Unsurprisingly, she denies having anything to do with Dev's death,' he went on. 'And she gave us an alibi for her whereabouts that afternoon that can be checked, but even if someone else did the actual deed, it's possible that she helped them by making the medicine available. She seemed very nervous when Hebden and I questioned her.'

'Have you arrested her?'

'No, but I've told her she mustn't speak to anyone about this. To be on the safe side, I'd be grateful if you'd move her to other accommodation, away from the guest area of the hotel, and have her meals brought to the room. I've told her it's for her own safety, but more to the point, if she's involved, I want to minimise her chances of tipping anyone off.'

The telephone rang and Sanjeewa picked up the receiver. 'Gunesekera here.'

It was a brief conversation. As he replaced the receiver in its cradle, Sanjeewa shook his head. 'There's nothing in the maintenance book and no one remembers hearing about an electrical problem on that corridor, or indeed anywhere else in the hotel in the last week. Either Nurse Collins is lying, and she's invented this maintenance man to cover her tracks—'

'Or she's innocent and the murderer impersonated a member of your staff.'

'When are you going to tell the rest of the family? It will come as a shock to them.' He paused and frowned. 'But I suppose one can't discount the possibility that one of them already knows.'

'Indeed. I'd like to deal with Nurse Collins first though. I need to take her down to the police station to take her fingerprints and find out if anyone else's are on the medicine bottle. Hers will be there of course because she brought the bottle out and showed it to us. There were none on the syringe. It would be a great help if you'd check out her alibi for me. She claims she was by the pool all afternoon and there were various pool attendants and guests who saw her.'

'I'll see to it.'

'I'll send my sergeant and my constable to check her room for fingerprints, but that may have to wait until tomorrow. Do you know where the electricity supply to her room is controlled from?'

'There's a cupboard at the far end of the corridor. All of the hotel's bedroom areas are wired in that way. It ensures that the maintenance people disrupt the supply as little as possible if there's a problem.'

'I'll have Prasanna and Nadar look in there too.'

'Nurse Collins' room has been the only one on the corridor to be occupied for the last few days. It will be easy to put the area out of bounds if you wish me to.'

'Yes, please. And anything you can discreetly find out about the rest of the family's whereabouts that afternoon would be very useful. But don't tell them about this development. I'll do that when I'm ready to speak to them. I'll come back once I've finished at the station.'

'Hopefully, I'll have some information for you by then.'

'Good man,' said de Silva, feeling somewhat sorry for his beleaguered friend.

CHAPTER 15

De Silva drove Nurse Collins back to the hotel a couple of hours later. He had decided not to challenge her story for the moment. On arrival at the Crown, a chambermaid helped her to pack, and she was shown to her new room. She was still very subdued. There had been only one set of fingerprints on the bottle: her own.

'Nothing to help us there,' said de Silva when he was back with Sanjeewa. 'Do you have any news for me?'

'I've made some progress. I used the excuse that there was confusion over some bills, and the hotel's resident masseuse and our hairdresser confirmed that Sunita and Layla Khan had appointments that afternoon. I thought I'd try them first as I know Sunita often uses their services.' He raised an eyebrow. 'They remembered as soon as I asked. They'd previously been booked by Mrs Patel, but she cancelled at short notice, so they were free when Sunita requested them. She's a much more popular client. As you might guess, I wasn't surprised to hear that Mrs Patel's difficult. Our hairdresser told me he wasn't looking forward to the appointment. Apparently, she's hard to please and complains at the slightest thing. Her hair is equally difficult. He described styling it to her satisfaction as being like trying to make a river flow uphill.'

'What about Nurse Collins' alibi?'

'Two of the pool attendants saw her there from around

midday and she didn't depart until teatime. Do you want me to try to find out where the rest of the party were?'

'Thank you, but now I'm back, I'll take over from here. Do you know if any of them are in the hotel at the moment?'

Sanjeewa reached for the telephone. 'I'll see what I can find out. Are you still going to hold back the information that you think Dev was murdered?'

'Yes. I'd like to see the report from the laboratory and the result of the autopsy first, but it will do no harm to have a general word with them.'

A few calls established that Raj Khan was at the swimming pool, but no one knew where Salman had got to. Ashok was also out, seeing off the last few truckloads of the film company's equipment to Colombo.

'He seems to be in charge of everything,' said Sanjeewa. 'Presumably the director, Hari Bedu, receives the equipment and does whatever's necessary at that end.'

'How are Dev's wife and daughter?'

'They've hardly left their suites.'

'I think I'll leave speaking to them for a while and make a start with Raj. As I don't want to show my hand at this stage, I hope he'll believe me when I say I just need to ask him a few questions as a formality. Do you know much about him?'

'Apart from good looks, his most marked characteristic seems to be a very high opinion of himself. I doubt he possesses a particularly inquiring mind. Do you want me to send someone to fetch him up here? I can reserve one of the small lounges for you.'

De Silva paused then shook his head. 'Thank you, but I'd rather the meeting didn't appear too formal. I'll go down to the pool and speak to him there.'

* * *

The Crown Hotel was the only one in Nuala that boasted a swimming pool. Indeed, as far as de Silva was aware, there were only a handful in the area's private homes. Its blue water gleamed in the late afternoon sunshine. On the paved area surrounding it, there were rows of navy-and-white-striped loungers shaded by large orange parasols fringed with white tassels. Only a few of the loungers were occupied.

De Silva recognised Raj straight away. He wore red-and-white check swimming trunks and a pair of expensive-looking dark glasses. His bare torso displayed an enviable set of muscles and his skin glistened with suntan oil. To all appearances, he hadn't a care in the world.

On the next-door lounger sat a glamorous young woman dressed in a yellow gingham two-piece bathing costume, dark glasses, and a yellow sunhat. A burst of laughter from Raj at some remark she made drifted across the lawn. De Silva wondered if she was also in the film business. He was pretty sure that attitudes in India were the same as those in Ceylon, where her outfit would be too daring for most women to wear.

By the time de Silva reached the two of them, Raj had shifted position to lie on his back, his hands interlaced behind his head. He looked to be planning to go to sleep, and his companion had picked up a fashion magazine and was flipping through its pages in a desultory manner. De Silva cleared his throat and she glanced up at him with a bored expression on her face. Lazily, Raj uncoupled his hands, pinched the frame of his dark glasses between his thumb and forefinger, and lifted them a fraction. He regarded de Silva with a hint of displeasure.

'Forgive me for disturbing you, Mr Khan. Please accept my condolences on the death of your stepfather.'

'Thank you.'

'I wonder if you'd spare me a few moments?'

'What for?'

'I'd be grateful for your help.'

'Really? And who are you?'

'Inspector de Silva, chief of the Nuala police.'

'I hadn't heard this was a police matter. My stepfather died of heart failure.'

'Of course, but as there was no medical practitioner present at the time, there needs to be an inquest. It's customary for the police to make a report to the coroner. It's merely a formality.'

Raj gave a grunt of assent. His companion put down her magazine, swung her long, slim legs off the lounger and stood up. 'I think I'll go for a stroll and leave you to talk.' Her voice had a seductively husky tone.

Raj smiled. 'You do that, darling. If the waiter comes by, shall I order us a sundowner?'

'Lovely.'

Briefly, Raj's eyes followed her as she walked away. De Silva couldn't resist doing the same then he heard Raj chuckle. 'Serious talk bores Rana. Shall we get this over with before she comes back?'

'Of course.' De Silva pulled out his notebook. 'In the days before your stepfather's death, do you recall any indications that his health was deteriorating?'

Raj shrugged. 'No. We all knew he had a weak heart, but his health was no worse than usual.'

'Was he under any particular strain?'

'Only the filming of the big scene the other evening.' He gave a dry smile. 'But Dev always made a fuss about how much pressure he was under. As usual, it went off without a hitch.'

'I hope you'll forgive me for bringing it up, but I've heard that he and your stepmother had a serious argument a few days ago. Did he say anything to you about being distressed by that?'

Raj's smile displayed brilliantly white, even teeth. 'Distressed? Infuriated is more the word I'd use. Sunita can be a firebrand, but after the years they've been married, he was used to it. He liked drama in his life. I doubt he'd have been happy with a woman who agreed with him all the time. Neither of them liked to be the first to offer to make up, but they always did, even if it took a few days.'

'May I ask where you were on the afternoon he died?'

Raj frowned. 'Why do you ask?'

'Only to complete the record.'

'I breakfasted at the hotel then Rana and I took a drive in the country. We'd been invited to a lunch party by the owners of one of the plantations near here.'

'May I ask their name?'

Raj looked surprised but he gave it. 'We'd planned to return the same evening,' he went on, 'but the party was lively. It grew late, and rather than negotiate country roads in the dark, our hosts invited us to stay overnight.'

A waiter with a white napkin draped over one arm approached them. 'Would you like to order something, sahib?' he asked.

'Yes, two rum punches. Will you have a drink, Inspector?'

'Thank you, but no.'

'On duty, eh?' He paused as the waiter cleared the empty glasses from the table next to his lounger. 'I hope I'm not being accused of anything,' he said with a dry smile when the waiter had gone.

De Silva felt a prickle of discomfort. Perhaps the actor wasn't as lacking in perception as Sanjeewa judged him to be. He hoped he hadn't overplayed his hand. 'Not at all, sir,' he said quickly. 'This must be a very sad time for your family.'

'Yes, understandably Sunita is very distressed, and so is Layla. She was always his favourite, although he and I rubbed along pretty well.' Raj's matter-of-fact tone suggested that he didn't resent his stepsister.

'What about your brother?'

'Sal!' Raj raised his eyes to heaven. 'Much as I love my brother, I can't ignore his weaknesses. He never stood up to Dev. If you wanted a man like my stepfather to respect you, you had to stand up to him. Make him see that you were as good as he was.'

'How has he taken the news?'

'As I've not seen him, I couldn't say,' said Raj with a shrug.

'I understand that your brother isn't an actor.'

'No, he's a writer.'

'What did he and your stepfather disagree about?'

'Oh, the way the film business is going. My stepfather's ambition was always to make spectacular films. He said historical epics were what the public wanted to see.'

'And your brother?'

'He sees a different way forward. Films that deal with modern life.' Raj laughed. 'With respect to my stepfather's memory, the idea is appealing. Sal writes well, and sometimes I feel that I've spent enough years playing the swashbuckling roles, trussed up in armour and sandals, with all that sword fighting. A different style of acting that displays the wider range of my talents would make a pleasant change.'

As Sanjeewa had observed, Raj didn't suffer from false modesty, thought de Silva.

'I appreciate these are early days, but do you intend to continue with the film?'

'There'll have to be some rewriting but most of the scenes have been completed. I'm taking charge of all that. Sunita and Layla don't have the experience and Sal isn't the right man for the job.'

'What about Ashok Mehta?'

Raj gave a dismissive wave of the hand. 'I'll keep him on, but he's not one of the family.'

But he's the one who's still seeing to the business of the company, thought de Silva, *whilst you're enjoying yourself by the pool.*

He asked a few more questions, then when the waiter arrived with the drinks, put away his notebook. 'Thank you for your time, and once again, please accept my condolences.'

'You're very kind.'

De Silva walked away, but just before he left the pool enclosure, he turned to look back. Raj's girlfriend had returned to the lounger and her magazine. Raj sat beside her, staring into the distance, slowly sipping his rum punch.

* * *

Inside the hotel, de Silva was passing through the lobby on his way out to the Morris when he noticed that Sanjeewa was once more occupied with Mrs Patel. He wondered what had annoyed her this time. As she talked, she prodded his friend in the chest as if he was a stallholder in the bazaar who'd tried to palm her off with a piece of inferior meat. He would have liked a word with Sanjeewa but obviously now wasn't the time. He'd call him when he got back to the station to ask if he'd get in touch when Ashok and Salman returned to the hotel. Salman's absence in particular troubled him. Raj didn't seem to find anything odd about it, but was there more to it than met the eye? If he didn't turn up soon, he'd have to organise a search.

On the way out, he met Ashok coming up the steps.

'Good afternoon, Inspector. Were you looking for me?'

'There's no hurry,' said de Silva, not wanting to raise the young man's suspicions, 'but since you're here, it would be helpful if you'd confirm a few details for my report to the coroner. As you may be aware, it's customary for there to be an inquest in situations where no medical practitioner was present at the time of a death.'

'Of course. I would have contacted you myself, but I've been out since breakfast, organising the shipment of the last of our equipment to Colombo.'

'So the manager told me.'

'I didn't want to leave Sunita and Layla but there wasn't much choice. Have you spoken with them today?'

'I didn't want to intrude.'

'I see.' Ashok gestured to the hotel entrance. 'Would you like to go inside?'

De Silva thought of the lobby and Mrs Patel. Sanjeewa would probably still be too busy with her to find them a quiet room, and he preferred not to have a conversation in public.

'Shall we take a walk instead?' He pointed to the archway to one side of the drive that he knew led to a quiet part of the gardens.

Ashok looked slightly surprised, but he nodded.

Gravel crunched under their feet as they followed the path that led to the hotel's Italian garden. It was enclosed by walls of weathered stone and filled with a maze created out of low box hedging. A fountain with a stone nymph holding an amphora stood in the centre. Water cascaded from it, sparkling in the sunshine. The style of the garden had never been to de Silva's taste; he preferred colourful flowers, but he appreciated the amount of work that must be needed to preserve the elegant effect.

'This inquest,' said Ashok. 'I hope the formalities can be completed quickly. It will only be a small step towards coming to terms with what's happened, but I think it might help Sunita and Layla if they have the funeral behind them.'

De Silva noticed that he didn't mention Raj or Salman.

'Of course. I'll do my best to expedite matters. Archie Clutterbuck acts as coroner in Nuala and I'm sure he too will do everything in his power to avoid unnecessary delay.'

'So what were these questions you wanted to ask me?'

'Mainly I wanted to be sure that you have nothing to add to the information you've already given.'

'I can't think of anything.'

'I spoke earlier with Raj Khan but I've yet to meet his brother Salman and take a statement from him. Does he know his stepfather is dead?'

'I'm not sure. I didn't see him on the afternoon Dev died and I've not seen him since.'

'Do you think he'll be very distressed by the news?'

'It's hard to say. He and Dev didn't always get on, but inevitably, his death means that everything will be turned upside down. And even in good times, Salman doesn't find life easy.'

He gave a wry smile. 'Something for which Dev had little sympathy. He was fond of saying he was brought up in the school of hard knocks and it did him no harm. But Salman has a good heart. I'm sure that given time, he'll do his best to help Raj to keep the company going. Maybe he'll try to help Sunita too. She's never taken an active part in running the company and now that Raj will be stepping into Dev's shoes, her position will be less secure. Several times, I've heard Raj complain that she's getting too old for the parts she wants to play. Salman's also very fond of Layla who's devastated by her father's death.'

'Do you have any idea where Salman's gone?'

'No.' A suspicious expression came over Ashok's face. 'What are you suggesting, Inspector?'

'I was just thinking of his safety,' said de Silva hurriedly.

'Very laudable. But I doubt he'll come to any harm. He goes off on his own quite often. If there's nothing else you wanted to discuss, shall we go back?'

CHAPTER 16

'I haven't spoken to all of the family yet,' said de Silva as he and Jane ate a much-delayed supper.

Their cook had rustled up baked eggs, spiced cauliflower patties, and grilled paneer in curry sauce, followed by slices of fresh mango. De Silva had explained about the finding of the syringe and the new light it cast on Dev's death and had given Jane the gist of the conversation he and David Hebden had with Anne Collins, and his own with Raj Khan.

'Dev's wife and daughter both have a good alibi,' he went on. 'The hotel's masseuse and its hairdresser confirmed that they were with them on the afternoon Dev died. They'll have to be told eventually that Dev didn't die of natural causes, but I think it can wait for a while longer. Hopefully giving them more time to recover from the shock of his death will help a little. Anne Collins is safe for the moment, and she also has an alibi for the time of Dev's death. There were no fingerprints on the syringe and the only set on the bottle belongs to her. She handled it in Hebden's and my presence. Hebden didn't touch it. I only did so with a handkerchief around my hand.'

'I expect that an accomplice or a thief would probably wipe the bottle clean before they replaced it.'

'No doubt. I'm going to send Prasanna and Nadar up to the Crown to go thoroughly over the room for fingerprints but I'm not optimistic they'll find anything that will provide a clue as to who the murderer was. I've yet to check out Raj's alibi but it will probably be watertight.'

'I suppose it could be argued that he was behind Dev's death and used someone else to do his dirty work. The same might apply to Sunita and Layla.'

De Silva shrugged. 'Yes, but otherwise, we're left with two suspects who may or may not have been helped by Collins: the stepson Salman and Ashok Mehta. Salman is missing and I only have Ashok's word for his movements that afternoon.'

Jane frowned. 'If Dev bullied Salman, as his brother indicated to you, that would give him a motive, but do you think he's the kind of person who would commit murder?'

'It's surprising what even the gentlest of people can be driven to if there's sufficient provocation. And so far, we have no idea whether he has an alibi.'

'What about Ashok? There was that conversation you overheard him having with Layla.'

'Yes, I have to consider him, and the possibility that she knew what he was planning.'

They were silent for a few moments until Jane spoke. 'Going back to Nurse Collins, it does seem odd that when this maintenance man asked her to leave her door open, she forgot to ask how he was going to lock it afterwards. One would think it was something she'd want to be sure he did.'

'Yes. As I said to David Hebden, if she was telling the truth about forgetting to ask him, it shows a great disregard for security.'

'And if he had a spare key to lock the door, why did he need her to leave it open in the first place?'

'Quite'

'After what Sanjeewa told you, are you going to question her again?'

'Not yet.'

'So what do you intend to do next?'

De Silva folded his napkin and dropped it on the table. 'In the morning, I must go up to the Residence to see Archie. I rang him earlier to tell him the news and make him aware that I planned to involve Sanjeewa in the investigation as he has the inside track where the hotel's concerned. He agreed but we only spoke briefly as he had important guests, so I need to tell him the rest of what I've found out.'

'How did he take the news?'

'Pretty badly at first, but he calmed down. He also accepted Sanjeewa's involvement.' He got up. 'Before I go to bed, I'd like to spend a little while on the verandah enjoying some peace. Will you join me?'

'That would be nice.'

'I think I'm going to have a nightcap. Would you like something too?'

'Well, I don't usually, but this evening a drop of that cherry brandy that the Hebdens gave us for Christmas would be very nice.'

Followed by Jane, de Silva went into the drawing room and poured a liqueur glass of cherry brandy for her and a whisky for himself. He smelled the sweet, syrupy richness of the brandy.

Out on the verandah the air, perfumed by the scent of jasmine, had cooled to a perfect temperature. Stars glittered above them. Billy and Bella soon appeared. Bella jumped onto de Silva's lap and curled up in a ball.

This was just what he needed, he mused, stroking the little cat's glossy black fur: time to relax and collect his thoughts. He feared this wasn't going to be an easy case. After what Hebden had said about the difficulty of identifying digitoxin in a corpse, there was little point placing much reliance on the outcome of the autopsy. Of course, there was still the residue in the syringe, but even though it might turn out to be digitoxin and provide evidence that Dev had been murdered, it wouldn't point the finger at the murderer.

Some cases turned on the criminal making an unforced mistake, but where Ashok was concerned, de Silva suspected the chances of that were remote. He was a clever young man. If challenged, he might simply deny the words de Silva had heard at the cricket club or claim all he'd meant was that he and Layla should run away together.

His thoughts turned to Raj's alibi. That needed to be verified. If it was watertight, it made Salman the most likely suspect out of the brothers. His difficult relationship with Dev gave him a motive and, with or without Nurse Collins' help, he might have had the means. His absence indicated that he'd had the opportunity too. It was extremely suspicious that he'd disappeared, apparently without a word to anyone.

'You're very quiet, Shanti,' said Jane. 'Mind whirring?'

He let out a long sigh. 'I'm sorry, I'm not very good company tonight.'

'Gracious, you've no need to apologise.'

'It's just that there are a number of possibilities to consider, and at the moment, none of them stand out as far more likely solutions to the case than the others.' He gave her a rueful smile.

'I'm sure everything will fall into place soon.'

'I hope you're right Anyway, tomorrow I'll make a start by organising a search for Salman. I remember Ashok saying something about photographers taking pictures of the family at the hotel. Maybe there'll be one of Salman that I can get hold of discreetly.'

CHAPTER 17

The following morning, after he'd told them about his last conversation with Nurse Collins and her story about the maintenance man, de Silva sent Prasanna and Nadar to the Crown to check her room and the electricity cupboard for fingerprints. He was alone at the station waiting to hear from Archie's secretary when Hebden called.

'The laboratory identified the residue in the syringe as digitoxin, but as I feared, the pathologist who carried out the autopsy wasn't able to detect any in the body. However, his report does contain something of interest.'

De Silva waited expectantly.

'He found a needle mark on the body. The skin around it was badly discoloured, and it was in Khan's left thigh. The amount of bruising and the unorthodox position suggests that an injection was forced on him, possibly by someone not used to giving them. Anyway, didn't Nurse Collins tell us that she gave him his medication orally because he had a horror of needles?'

'Yes, she did.'

'Have you got anywhere with the rest of the family?'

Briefly, de Silva outlined the information he had from Sanjeewa regarding Sunita and Layla as well as his conversations with Raj and Ashok. 'Especially after what you've told me,' he added, 'I want to speak to Salman Khan as soon as possible.'

'He can't have vanished into thin air.'

'No, but he might have left Nuala. I think it's time I alerted other forces to be on the lookout.'

'Is Archie in the know?'

'He knows Dev was murdered, but I'm waiting to see him to tell him the rest. His secretary should be telephoning me to let me know when he'll see me.'

'I'll get off the phone then. Good luck.'

* * *

The call from the Residence came shortly afterwards. De Silva locked up and set off. He decided against leaving a note for Prasanna and Nadar. It would be easier to explain what Hebden had told him in person.

As he drove through town, he remembered the pay rise Prasanna and Nadar were hoping for. Unfortunately, this probably wasn't the time to remind Archie that he'd promised to come to a decision soon. They might have to be patient until the Khan case was resolved.

His boss greeted him sombrely and listened as he explained about his investigations so far and the circumstances surrounding Dev's death.

'So,' said Archie when he'd finished. 'Just to be sure I've got all this straight. This so-called maintenance man that the nurse claims to have met that evening would have had the opportunity to get into her room after she went down for dinner. Once inside, there was nothing to stop him gaining access to Dev's heart medicine. It appears that some of it and possibly one of her syringes were taken. Hebden confirms that an excessive dose of the medicine, given by injection, would kill the recipient very quickly. Despite there being no trace of it found when the body was examined, that's not unusual, but there was a fresh needle mark.'

'That's correct, sir.'

'And are you convinced that Dev didn't do away with himself?'

'Yes. I'm satisfied he wouldn't have injected the medication himself. He had a horror of needles.'

'Then who do you have in mind as suspects? Putting aside the matter of this maintenance man, members of the family are usually the first people to consider, aren't they?'

'I can't point to any of them not being implicated, but I think his wife and daughter are the least likely. They both have solid alibis for the afternoon he died. By all accounts his daughter, Layla, was devoted to him.'

Archie frowned. 'Are you implying his wife wasn't?'

'I understand they argued a great deal, but always made up. According to the stepson Raj, they thrived on it.'

'I'm more for the quiet life, myself, and I imagine you agree,' said Archie with a smile.

'I do.'

'Carry on.'

'Dev didn't get on well with either of his stepsons, although I believe Raj coped better with his overbearing ways than Salman did.'

'That doesn't surprise me. My wife and I met Raj at that do after the filming. Full of himself, I thought. A good-looking chap and knew it. I don't recall a brother.'

'Apparently, he's a very different character. Much more self-effacing. I've spoken to Raj and will check out his alibi for the afternoon, but at the moment, I haven't mentioned there's evidence that their stepfather was murdered. Salman hasn't been seen since Dev was killed.'

'Hmm, suspicious. You'd better mount a search for him.'

'I have that in hand,' said de Silva, allowing himself some latitude. After all, he soon would.

'Anyone else on the list?'

'His assistant, Ashok Mehta.'

'What would be in it for him?'

As de Silva explained about the conversation he'd overheard, Archie scratched his florid cheek. 'Might be an innocent remark,' he said eventually. 'What about an alibi? Didn't he say he was working in his room until he broke off to look for Dev? Can anyone corroborate that?'

'Sanjeewa Gunesekera may be able to help on that score. Someone on his staff might have noticed Ashok leaving the hotel earlier than he claimed to have done.'

'Tricky one. Well, you'd better deal with the alibis first. Can't go around arresting people on flimsy evidence, especially if they may be involved with a close relation of the deceased. That would really set the cat among the pigeons with the family. And I don't want any sloppiness in this investigation. Things could get much worse if the press sniff out that something's wrong.'

His boss's critical insinuation and harsh tone irritated de Silva, but he schooled himself to be patient.

Archie ran a hand through his thinning hair. 'Apologies,' he said gruffly. 'I know you don't need me to tell you how to run your case and I appreciate your keeping me informed.' He fell silent and the glum expression on his face made de Silva wonder if there was something more than the danger of publicity troubling him. It also occurred to him that it was odd that Darcy hadn't got up to come and greet a visitor as he normally did, just remained close to his master's chair, with Archie leaning down from time to time to give him a reassuring pat.

'Is there anything else you'd like to discuss, sir?' he asked.

Archie sighed. 'To tell you the truth there is. Before this blew up, I was going to ask you for your opinion on a spot of bother we're having up here.'

'I'll be glad to help in any way I can.'

'The truth is, it's preying on my mind.'

De Silva waited for him to go on.

'It started a couple of days ago. One of the servants let Darcy out just after dawn to do his morning business but a minute or two later, he came pelting back in a hell of a state. The servant called me, and I managed to calm him down, but since then, he won't go outside unless I'm with him.' Archie stood up. 'Let me show you.'

He went to the door that led into the garden, opened it, and stepped outside. Darcy, who had followed him, hung back, his tail wagging uncertainly. He emitted a low whine.

Archie bent forward and slapped his knees with the palms of his hands. 'Come on, old chap, out you come. Nothing to be afraid of.'

Darcy took a few steps towards him then stopped. The whine grew louder.

A note of exasperation entered Archie's voice. 'Darcy! Come along with you!'

Reluctantly, Darcy crossed the threshold and followed Archie a little way into the garden but as soon as he started to come back, the dog streaked past him with a turn of speed de Silva hadn't seen in years.

'Do you think he might have met a predator?' he asked when Archie had sat down again with Darcy wedged tightly to the side of his chair.

'That was my first thought, but the servants have scoured the grounds and found no sign of tracks or droppings.' Archie shook his head. 'Whatever's causing his behaviour has me flummoxed. He's never been like it before. Even when I take him shooting, he doesn't turn a hair.'

'Very strange, I agree. If whatever alarmed him only appears at dawn, all I can suggest is that a watch is put on the grounds around that time. Perhaps my sergeant and my constable could help.'

'Let's see what transpires,' said Archie, 'I'll let you know if I want their help.'

*   *   *

'How did you get on with Archie?' asked Jane when de Silva stopped off at Sunnybank for a quick lunch of rice with a jackfruit curry and to bring her up to date.

'I'd heard from David Hebden before I saw him. I was right about the substance in the syringe being digitoxin and there was a fresh injection mark on the body. I've told Archie everything I've discovered so far. Naturally he's not happy about the situation, especially when there might be interest from the newspapers, but on the plus side, he agreed to Sanjeewa helping me.'

'Good. What's next?'

'Prasanna and Nadar are checking Nurse Collins' room for fingerprints. Although between us Sanjeewa and I have established that Sunita, Layla, and Raj Khan have alibis, I still need to check Raj's. That will be easier than verifying Ashok's story. I'll start a search for Salman if he hasn't turned up at the hotel already. I'm hoping to find a photograph of him that I can send out to other police forces.'

'I may be able to help there,' said Jane. 'I think there was an article in the *Nuala Times* the other day that had some photographs of the Khans in it. Shall I see if I can find it? Salman might be in some of them.'

'Thank you. Oh, I haven't told you about the other problem. If you've heard about it from Florence, you didn't mention it.'

'What problem?'

He explained about the mysterious intruder at the Residence.

'Poor Archie,' said Jane when he'd finished. 'He's devoted to that dog. There's definitely something odd going on at the Residence. Did I tell you about Florence's spectacles?'

'No.'

Jane recounted the story. 'And since then,' she went on,

'other things have gone missing. She mentioned it at this week's sewing circle meeting.'

'Such as?'

'A teaspoon from a set she's fond of. It was with some cups and saucers laid out ready for tea in the garden. The set has tiny replicas of tea flower buds at the end of each teaspoon handle. It's very unusual.'

De Silva frowned. 'Was she sure that one of the servants hadn't just put the wrong number out?'

'She did think of that, but she made them check the overall number of spoons in the cutlery canteen and the set was one short.'

'Ah well.' De Silva yawned. He found it difficult to get worked up over teaspoons, however pretty and unusual they might be. 'I'd better be off to the station. I hope Prasanna and Nadar will be back from the Crown and I've yet to tell them the latest news. After that I'll go up to this plantation where Raj Khan says he attended a lunch party on the day Dev was found dead.'

'Won't it be rather awkward if he finds out you've been asking questions?'

'I hope he won't. But of course, if it looks as if he's the guilty party, I'll have to confront him eventually.'

De Silva dabbed his mouth with his napkin. 'That jackfruit was delicious.' He dropped the napkin on the table. 'Now, I really must be going.'

Jane laughed.

'What is it?'

She tapped a finger to her chin, 'You missed a bit.'

De Silva raised a smile as he retrieved the napkin and wiped away the offending speck of sauce. 'It's good that I have you to keep me looking presentable.'

'Of course.'

* * *

At the station, Prasanna and Nadar had returned and he called them into his office.

'Anything to report?' he asked.

'No, sir. We went over everything as thoroughly as possible. The only fingerprints in the room matched the nurse's ones. There were none at all in the electricity cupboard. In fact, it looked as if no one had been into it for a long time. There was a thick layer of dust on most of the surfaces.'

'Right, well done, both of you. Now, Doctor Hebden has given me some interesting news. As anticipated, the autopsy didn't reveal any digitoxin in Dev's body, but the laboratory confirmed that there was residue in the syringe. There was also a fresh needle mark on the body. I believe we can be sure that we have a murder on our hands.'

'Who do you suspect, sir?' asked Prasanna.

'I believe that Dev's wife and daughter have good alibis, so perhaps one of his stepsons. Raj claims to have been at a party in the hills from the morning of Dev's death until the next day but I need to verify that. Then in view of the conversation I mentioned to you that I overheard, I still have to consider Ashok Mehta. And we need to find Raj's brother, Salman. Once I have a photograph of him, I'd like the two of you to start looking around town and get out a search request to the other local forces for me. It continues to be very important to keep this whole matter quiet, so you must stress there's to be no publicity.'

He paused. 'You look thoughtful, Prasanna.'

'I was just remembering something we heard when we stayed on after the filming that night.'

'Yes?'

'Some of the extras who played the palace guards were telling stories about the actors. One of them told us that there was a time when Raj got very friendly with Nurse Collins. His girlfriend Rana knew nothing about it.'

De Silva's brow furrowed. 'That's most interesting,' he

said slowly. 'Thank you. When I get back from the plantation, I'll have another talk with Nurse Collins.'

CHAPTER 18

The road up to the plantation was steep and winding, revealing one breathtaking view after another. The first sight de Silva had of the plantation house was its long terracotta roof, a sharp contrast to the vivid green of the tea bushes cloaking the hill on which it stood. In April, it was coming towards the end of the dry season in the hill country. Workers were busy with late harvesting.

A drive lined with banks of rhododendrons and oleanders led to the house. It was an impressive building, its white-painted frontage punctuated alternately by balconies and deep verandahs, creating a pleasing juxtaposition of light and shade. Large copper pots filled with lilies and cannas stood against the walls beneath the windows.

De Silva parked the Morris and got out. The air was cooler up here than down in Nuala. It had to be one of the highest spots in the area. He went up to the front door and rang the bell. A few moments passed before a servant opened the door. If the sight of a policeman on the doorstep surprised him, he didn't show it.

'Good afternoon,' said de Silva. 'I'd like to see your master or mistress.'

'Sahib is down at the factory, but the memsahib is here.'

'Good, please tell her my name is Inspector de Silva of the Nuala police. I'll try not to take up too much of her time.'

The servant nodded. 'I will tell her.'

He showed de Silva into the hall then disappeared for a brief time. Whilst he waited, de Silva admired his surroundings. The hall was elegantly proportioned with an intricate parquet floor that combined honey-coloured and dark wood. An impressive staircase took up most of its left-hand side. On the opposite wall, there were two beautifully carved rosewood chairs with high backs and a table with a marble top. Numerous silk hangings depicting exotic plants and mythical creatures in jewel-bright colours hung on the walls.

'The memsahib asks you to join her on the terrace,' said the servant when he reappeared. De Silva followed him down a corridor that led towards the rear of the house. As they emerged onto the terrace, he couldn't help pausing. The view was magnificent, encompassing such a panorama that for a moment he had the sensation that if he launched himself out into it, he would be able to soar over the green hills.

'Good afternoon, Inspector,' said a melodious voice. Quickly, he pulled himself back to the job in hand.

'Thank you for sparing your time, ma'am.'

Mrs Faulkner smiled. She looked to be in her mid-thirties, elegantly dressed in a sea-green silk dress and matching sandals. Her blonde hair was tied back from her face by a folded green scarf. 'It's no trouble, although I am rather mystified as to why you want to see me. If it's a business matter, I'm afraid you'll have to wait for my husband to come home.'

'It's not a business matter, ma'am.'

'You intrigue me even more, Inspector. Do sit down and reveal all. May I offer you some refreshment first? Iced tea perhaps?'

'You're very kind, that would be most welcome.'

She beckoned to the servant who hovered in the

background and ordered the tea. 'So,' she said when the man had gone, 'shall we get on to the reason why you're here?'

'I understand you held a lunch party recently.'

'That's right. We entertained about thirty guests.'

'Was one of them the actor Raj Khan?'

She nodded. 'He came with his girlfriend. My husband and I met them when we were dining at the Crown one evening. They were good company, and we thought it would be amusing for our other guests to have a celebrity at the party.'

'Do you remember what time they arrived?'

Mrs Faulkner considered for a moment. 'Shortly before midday. We planned to have drinks here on the terrace before lunching at half past one.'

'At what time did the party break up?'

'Most of the guests left before dark. The drive down from the house is hazardous at night so people usually prefer to negotiate it whilst it's still light. Raj and his girlfriend stayed on, however. In the end they left the following morning.'

'Was there any particular reason for that?'

Mrs Faulkner smiled. 'I wish I could say it was simply because they were having a good time, but unfortunately it wasn't that straightforward. I'm afraid there was a rather embarrassing incident—'

She broke off as the servant arrived with two tall glasses of iced tea on a tray. She waited until he'd gone before she continued. 'Raj had clearly been drinking before he arrived. I could smell alcohol on his breath. Behind the charm, his girlfriend seemed to be under considerable strain. His behaviour was bordering on surly. I began to wish I'd never invited him. Eventually she took me aside and apologised for his conduct. She told me he'd argued with his stepfather that morning and it always put him in a bad mood. She'd been anxious about coming to the party, but he'd refused to make their excuses. She thought it might help if he had a rest for a while, so I had a room prepared upstairs and she persuaded him to lie down.'

'Did she go with him?' De Silva took a sip of his iced tea.

'Briefly, but I'd already suggested that if he slept, she should join us for lunch. There was no point going hungry. She came back just as we were sitting down to our starters.'

'So, that would have been just after half-past one, am I right?'

'Yes.' She looked puzzled. 'What's this about, Inspector?'

'I'm afraid I'm not at liberty to go into detail, ma'am, but there are good reasons for my questions.'

Mrs Faulkner took a sip of her iced tea, and ice clinked against the side of the glass. 'Very well, I won't embarrass you by pressing the point.'

'Thank you. Do you remember what time Raj rejoined the party?'

'He arrived as we were finishing dessert. I suppose he'd been asleep about two and a half hours.'

'Would there have been servants on the drive or in the hall during the party?'

Again she looked puzzled. 'I doubt it. Once all the guests had arrived, they would have been helping to serve drinks and lunch.'

'One last question: how did he seem to you when he came back?'

'Completely different to when he arrived, thank goodness. He was charming and full of amusing anecdotes.'

'I'm glad to hear it. Thank you for your help. I'd be grateful if our conversation remained between ourselves.'

'Certainly.'

They chatted for a short while about the incredible view as de Silva finished his drink, then he took his leave. When he returned to the Morris, he looked at his watch. He'd also checked the time when leaving Nuala and on arrival at the plantation. The journey up had taken him forty minutes. The return one might be a little quicker as it would be downhill. It meant that if Raj had slipped out of the plantation house after his girlfriend returned to the lunch party, he would have had time to drive back to Nuala to meet his stepfather and kill him then return to the plantation before anyone noticed he'd been gone. Was it the case that he'd only pretended to be drunk to enable him to carry out that plan?

On the journey down to Nuala, de Silva was too preoccupied to enjoy the marvellous views spread out before him. He needed to revisit the place where Dev's body had been found to see if the timing added up. Raj would have taken too great a risk of being seen if he went through the hotel gardens to reach the place where Dev's body was found, so he would have needed to find a more discreet route. The extra time that might entail needed to be factored in.

If there was anything in his theory, de Silva wondered whether Raj's girlfriend had played a part. She was the most likely person to have checked on him whilst he was away from the rest of the party. Briefly, he considered questioning her but decided to wait. It was too soon to alert either of them to the way his mind was moving.

* * *

When he reached Nuala, he went straight to the Crown and headed across the garden to the place where Dev's body had been found, then started to explore the undergrowth bordering it. There was a narrow path that didn't appear to have been used for some time but was still just accessible. It brought him to a wall; he presumed it marked the garden boundary. The upper hinge of the door set into it had rusted and broken away from its fixings, leaving it hanging crooked. He crouched down for a better look and saw a flash of green as the lizard he'd disturbed scuttled away.

The door's leading edge had sunk about two inches into the soil and looked as if it had been there for some time. If Raj had come that way, de Silva very much doubted he'd used the door to get into the garden. He hauled himself back to his feet and surveyed the wall. Raj was a young man and gave the impression of being fit. He'd talked about the swashbuckling roles he was required to play, and no doubt he needed to train for them, so the climb might not present an insuperable problem.

De Silva put a hand on the brickwork and felt its warm, rough surface. In places the pointing had fallen out and the gaps might provide a few toeholds, but many of the bricks along the top were crumbling, only held together by ivy and clumps of grass. For a middle-aged detective who was a little too fond of his food, climbing it was going to be a hazardous business, but like it or not, if he was to investigate what was on the other side, he had to find a way.

All at once, he remembered Prasanna mentioning that there'd been some gardening tools and equipment in the shed. If he was lucky, the equipment might include a stepladder. He removed his jacket, rolled up his sleeves and walked back along the path.

The shed had no window, and it took a few moments for his eyes to become accustomed to the gloom before he saw a ladder in one corner, propped up behind two stacks of terracotta flowerpots. Carefully, he moved the pots aside and manoeuvred the ladder out. It was a solid wooden one and heavy. By the time he'd carried it out of the shed and returned to where he'd left his jacket, sweat was pouring down his face and sticking his shirt to his back.

He propped the ladder against the wall and considered his next move. With the ladder to help, the climb looked easier but still a challenge. All the same, he mustn't give up now.

When he'd wobbled the ladder about a bit, finding to his relief that it seemed sturdy enough, he put his foot on the first step. Cautiously, he moved slowly upwards, but he must have shifted his weight too fast for the ladder lurched to one side. He grabbed the top of the wall to steady himself, dislodging a few bricks and wincing as a falling one scraped his hand. His heart pounded and for a moment, it was a struggle to breathe.

After what seemed a far longer time than it probably was, his heart rate returned to its normal pace. He peered over the top of the wall. Mercifully, the ground on the other side was banked up against it and reasonably clear of vegetation. There was also no sign of snakes.

Once he had gone back to retrieve his jacket, he climbed the ladder again. He knocked away a stretch of loose bricks from the top of the wall, gritted his teeth and swung one leg over then hauled himself the rest of the way so that all his weight was on the top of the wall. Pain shot through him as he balanced there, then he let himself fall, landing in an ungainly heap on the other side. Before he could stop himself, he rolled down the small bank then sat at the bottom collecting his wits. A smile came over his face. The climb had been worth the effort. Through a sparse screen of trees, he saw a lane. He set off to investigate.

The lane was narrow, but the ground on either side of it was firm enough for a car to pull over and park. It took him about five minutes to reach another door into the hotel garden. This one was in better condition than the first although it was festooned with cobwebs. Of course, that didn't prove it hadn't been opened recently. Spiders were some of the fastest workers in the insect world. Several small rust-red ones scurried out as he parted the gauzy curtain to find the doorknob. Instinctively he tensed, remembering the old saying: the smaller the spider, the more poisonous it's likely to be, but to his relief, he didn't feel any stings. Soon he was through the door and back in the garden.

The walk back to the first door took only a few minutes. He returned the ladder to the shed and dusted himself off as best as he could. Now to work out whether it would make an appreciable difference to the time Raj needed if he had used this route to get into the garden, then he must speak to Sanjeewa.

CHAPTER 19

'I'm afraid I've still no news of Salman for you,' said Sanjeewa when de Silva was shown into his office. 'I would have been in touch if I had.' He looked more closely at his friend. 'Have you been running in a race?'

Shanti chuckled. 'No, climbing over your garden wall, but I'd hoped it wouldn't be too obvious that I've been exerting myself.'

'Maybe not to a casual observer although you might like to make use of one of the bathrooms before you meet anyone else. But I'm intrigued. Why were you climbing over our wall?'

De Silva explained about his visit to the Faulkners' plantation and his subsequent investigations. 'I think it's just possible Raj had time to meet his stepfather and kill him,' he went on. 'Doctor Hebden has confirmed that the substance in the syringe we found is digitoxin and there was a fresh puncture wound on the body indicating an injection. I'm even more convinced than I was previously that we have a murder on our hands.'

Sanjeewa frowned. 'I follow what you're saying, but Raj would need a strong nerve and some luck to succeed. Also, how would he get hold of the medicine and the syringe?'

'My sergeant and my constable were told by some of the film extras that he had an affair with Nurse Collins. If she still cares about him, she might have helped him.'

'And invented the story of the maintenance man to hide her actions?'

'Yes. I think I should question her again, don't you?'

Sanjeewa picked up the telephone receiver. 'I'll arrange it. I look forward to hearing what she has to say.'

'How has she been?'

'She's starting to complain about being prevented from leaving her room. In fact, I was thinking of telephoning you to ask if it was absolutely necessary to keep her there.'

'I may soon be able to give you the answer to that.'

'Are Raj and Salman now your only suspects?'

'No, there's Ashok too.'

Sanjeewa frowned. 'What would his motive be? Surely, he had a good job working for Dev. I know he could be demanding but Ashok seemed well able to handle him.'

'I haven't told you before, but I believe there's something between Ashok and Layla. A few days ago, I overheard him talking with her up at the film set. He said words to the effect that if they didn't do something, they'd never be free to be together. I think he may have meant that they needed to get rid of Dev.'

Sanjeewa looked shocked. 'Do you really think she'd agree to her father's murder? From what I saw, she was devoted to him, and he to her.'

'Jane said the same, but I don't think I should discount anything yet. Ashok claims to have been in his room working from the time when he left Dev after lunch until he went to find him to get the letters signed, but I've only his word for it. I'm also suspicious that he found Dev in such an out-of-the-way place. One explanation would be that he knew exactly where to go because he committed the crime himself.'

'Hmm, you have a point there.'

'It would help if you could discreetly find out from your staff if any of them noticed him leaving the hotel, and if so, what time it was.'

'Of course. I'll think of a way round it. What are you going to do about Salman?'

'I think it's time I involved other local police forces and began a proper search.'

'I'll continue to keep an eye out for him.'

'Thank you.'

* * *

There were shadows around Anne Collins' eyes, and she wore less makeup than she had done on the previous occasion that de Silva had seen her. There was, however, a look of steely determination on her face.

'I hope you've come to tell me I'm free to go, Inspector. I'm sure you're aware that unless you intend to charge me with something, you can't keep me here against my will forever.'

'I grant you that, ma'am, but as I said at our last meeting, for your own safety you'd be wise to remain.'

'Why? Who do you suggest will try to harm me?'

'I'm not at liberty to divulge any names, but the autopsy on the late Dev Khan's body has revealed that he received an injection that may well have led to his death. An injection of digitoxin. As you're aware, even a small overdose of the medicine is likely to be fatal.'

'What!' Her voice shook. 'Do you think the man I saw was responsible?'

'No, ma'am.'

'Then who?'

'Miss Collins, isn't it time you told me the truth?'

Her eyes widened. 'But I have—'

'My junior officers searched the cupboard where the switches for the supply are situated. There were no fingerprints there.'

'But there wouldn't be,' she said quickly. 'I'm sure the thief would have been careful to wipe any traces away.'

De Silva shook his head. 'There was no maintenance man, was there? The hotel manager spoke to the maintenance department for me. No problems with the electrical supply were reported that evening. No one was called to do any work. This maintenance man is a figment of your imagination, invented to cover up the fact that you gave the murderer the means to kill Dev Khan.'

Anne Collins' eyes flashed. 'How dare you! My job was to look after Dev and that's what I did.'

'Do you deny that you had an affair with his stepson Raj? We have evidence that he may have murdered his stepfather. Did he ask you to help him? Miss Collins, if you tell me the truth now, the courts may treat you leniently. I urge you not to hold anything back.'

Anne Collins hesitated for a moment. De Silva saw the conflict in her face. The knuckles of her clenched fists were white. He'd seen it many times: a woman led astray by her love for a man who callously used her to further his criminal ends. A woman so desperate to regain a man's love that she was prepared to risk her own future.

'I repeat,' he said quietly. 'Did Raj Khan ask you to help him kill his stepfather?'

Anne Collins went over to a chair and sat down heavily. She looked exhausted. 'No, he didn't, although I suspect he hated him. Dev could be a brute where both of the boys were concerned. I'm sure it was the reason Raj drank too much. He tried to pretend he didn't care what Dev thought of him, but I never believed that was true. I was always convinced that underneath the bravado, he cared very much.'

A hint of defiance flared in her eyes. 'I don't care if you believe me or not,' she said abruptly, 'but if Raj took the syringe and the medicine and used it to kill Dev, he did so without my knowledge.'

De Silva gave her a piercing look. 'Then how did he get into your room?'

A tear slipped down Anne Collins' cheek. 'He had a key. I gave it to him.' She wiped the tear away. 'He told me he was unhappy with Rana. He wanted us to be together, but he needed to wait for the right time to tell her it was over between them.' More tears brimmed. Her voice was husky. 'I've been a fool, haven't I?'

De Silva pitied her. He didn't believe she'd been a willing accomplice, and instinct told him that her grief was genuine. 'Any one of us can be tricked, ma'am,' he said gently.

'Are you going to arrest me?'

He shook his head. 'No, and if you really were unaware of what Raj may have planned, you have nothing to fear. But even so, I'd be failing in my duty if I didn't do everything in my power to ensure your safety. For that reason, I must insist that you remain where you are.'

CHAPTER 20

Back in Sanjeewa's office, de Silva recounted the gist of the interview.

'So, Raj may have had a motive and the means,' said Sanjeewa when he'd heard him out. 'And the timing allows for him to have met Dev that afternoon. Did Anne Collins convince you that she didn't know the syringe and medicine had been taken?'

De Silva nodded. 'Her story about why she'd let Raj keep a spare key to her room rang true. It makes me think that his girlfriend Rana is in the clear as well. I very much doubt he'd want her to ask questions about how he proposed to get hold of the syringe and the medicine. It would be extremely awkward explaining away why he still had a key to Anne Collins' bedroom.'

For a few moments, silence fell, broken by Sanjeewa. 'Well, are you going to arrest him?'

'Not yet. I'd like to have the last piece of the jigsaw in place before I show my hand.'

'And the last piece is?'

'Salman. Oh, by the way, did you find out anything about Ashok?'

'No, if he managed to leave the hotel that afternoon earlier than he admits to, he did so without being seen. I asked him about Salman, and he still claims not to know where he is. I had a word with Naseer Ansari, too in case he could help us but no luck. I'm afraid that I've run out of ideas.'

De Silva had to think hard before he remembered who Naseer Ansari was. 'Do you mean Dev's dresser?' he asked, picturing the old man with the limp, his leg having been crushed by a cartwheel, and the surprising speed at which his rolling gait carried him.

'Yes. He's still at the hotel, although the rest of the company have left for Colombo. Very cut up, poor fellow. He was genuinely fond of Dev. They knew each other from way back. He's afraid there'll be no place for him in the film company now Dev's gone.'

De Silva recalled Ashok telling him how Dev had helped Naseer when he was unable to work. 'Wouldn't the family keep him on out of loyalty to Dev's memory?'

'He has his doubts about Raj, although he has more faith in Salman. Apparently, he's always been good to him, but I gathered Naseer doesn't expect Salman to have much influence from now on. If he ever did.'

'Did he have an opinion on whether Sunita and Layla will help him?'

'Not really, but he told me he's always been fond of Layla.'

'And Sunita?'

'He wouldn't comment, and to me that spoke volumes.'

'How are they spending their time now?'

Sanjeewa shrugged. 'I can't say for sure. They don't come down from their rooms very often.'

*　*　*

'Are you surprised that none of the Khan party has asked where Anne Collins is?' asked Jane.

They sat on the verandah at Sunnybank after a late

dinner: a meal that included de Silva's favourite pea and cashew curry, spicy jackfruit, brinjal, and fragrant fluffy rice. It had left him feeling revived a little after the day's exertions.

'Not even Raj?' she went on. 'Surely if there's still something between them, he'd be curious to know why he's not seen her about in the hotel.'

De Silva shrugged. 'I agree it's rather strange, but then he may not want to draw attention to himself by asking after her. There's also the consideration that if he did make use of her feelings for him to steal the medicine and syringe, he may be afraid she's realised what he was up to and not want to face her. As for Sunita and Layla, Sanjeewa says they rarely leave their rooms. I expect Ashok reserves his concern for Layla. If any of them should happen to ask where Anne Collins has got to, Sanjeewa's promised to do his best to deflect their suspicion.'

'Well, I'm very relieved that you're safe after all your exertions to test Raj's alibi. You might have been badly hurt, you know, and it might have been a long time before anyone found you.'

'But I wasn't. In fact, I'm rather proud of myself that managed as well as I did.'

Jane smiled. 'I had a much less adventurous day, but I did find the photographs I promised to look for in the *Nuala Times*. I'll go and fetch the best one.'

A few minutes later she returned. 'Here you are,' she said handing him the cutting from the paper.

De Silva studied the photograph of Salman. 'Thank you, that will do very well. Prasanna and Nadar can get on with the job in the morning.'

The air was sweetly scented and balmy – it would be a few hours before the temperature plummeted. The sound of insects about their nightly business hummed like a distant engine. Billy sat at the top of the steps to the garden, batting at moths that came to the light, whilst Bella dozed contentedly on de Silva's lap. He stroked her ears, receiving a loud purr in return.

'Another reason Raj hasn't shown any interest in Anne Collins' whereabouts might be that despite his dubious alibi, he had nothing to do with his stepfather's death after all,' said Jane thoughtfully. 'He's put his relationship with her behind him and has no reason to be afraid.' She rested her chin on her hand. 'But then why keep the key?' she mused, half to herself.

'Absentmindedness?' suggested de Silva.

'Perhaps that's it. Particularly if he's self-centred. It may not have occurred to him that by holding on to it, he's encouraging her to keep her hopes alive. Charming people can be very callous about the effect they have on others.'

De Silva swirled the post-prandial whisky in his glass, savouring the rich, peaty aroma, then took another sip and gazed up at the sky. It was a cloudless night and the stars burned brightly in the velvety darkness, silent and peaceful, unlike the human ones that had come to Nuala and were causing a great deal of trouble. He went back to thinking about Raj. Should he discount him? he wondered. Surely it would be premature. He might be charming, but what had Shakespeare written? *One can smile and smile and be a villain.*

'Out of your three suspects,' said Jane, breaking in on his thoughts. 'To me, Salman seems the most likely murderer now. It's very odd to disappear like he has. When you find him, will you arrest him?'

'That will depend on what he has to say for himself, but I agree, he's not behaving like a man who has nothing to hide. The only innocent explanation would be that he has no idea what's happened, but his timing is suspicious.'

They sat in silence for a few moments. Billy lost interest in moths and began to wash one hind paw. De Silva always marvelled at the contortions into which the little cat was able to twist his sleek body.

'On another subject,' said Jane, 'Florence is still complaining about odd things happening at the Residence.'

'More teaspoons?' De Silva wished teaspoons were all he had to worry about. Perhaps when he retired, that would be the case. A little light police work might be pleasant as a change from his garden: a handkerchief missing from a washing line, a piece of unexplained burnt toast. Still, that happy prospect was a few years away.

'Shanti?'

He came back to what Jane was saying. 'Mmm?'

'I said even Angel has been affected now. He went missing when one of the servants was walking him. Florence was very upset and eventually she had a whole posse of servants searching. Apparently, some of them heard a terrific amount of barking then Angel rushed out of one of the wooded areas on the edge of the formal gardens and virtually leapt into one of the men's arms. The poor fellow was quite startled.'

De Silva was sure the man had been alarmed. Florence's beloved Shih Tzu, Angel, was a very different kind of dog to Archie's Darcy. Darcy was everyone's friend, but Angel was a feisty little creature.

'If this interloper, whatever or whoever it is, was able to frighten Angel, it must be formidable indeed,' he said. He wondered if the Residence's servants were already convinced of that and not making a serious effort to find the mystery visitor in the hope it would soon leave of its own accord.

'Florence is very annoyed that the mystery's not been solved yet. Mrs Peters suggested that she might consider leading a party of explorers herself.'

De Silva chuckled. He knew that the vicar's wife could be quite mischievous at times. Perhaps her position as the wife of a man of the cloth gave her a confidence that other ladies who were subordinate to Florence lacked. 'How did that go down?'

'Not well, but Mrs Peters didn't seem abashed. In her quiet way, she does tend to tease Florence.'

'A dangerous pursuit.'

'If the problem goes on much longer, it wouldn't surprise me if Florence doesn't ask you to get involved.'

He yawned. 'It wouldn't surprise me either. And I suppose I could hardly refuse. I did mention to Archie that I'd lend him Prasanna and Nadar if he wanted, but he hasn't followed it up. It's a pity as it would be excellent experience for them, and they've already shown a talent for finding things.'

'Why don't I telephone Florence and say you'll send them anyway?'

'Not yet, it will have to wait until they're not busy organising the search for Salman. I'll have to think over how to go about finding this interloper too. If we're dealing with an animal of some kind, it's more likely to carry out its raids when the Residence grounds are quiet. At dawn perhaps.'

'Very well, I'll leave it up to you.' Silence fell for a few moments, broken by Jane. 'How's Sanjeewa coping? It must be worrying for him to have such an unpleasant occurrence at the hotel.'

'Actually, I think that in a strange way he's rather enjoying it. The puzzle, not Dev's death I mean, and provided of course that the story doesn't get out amongst the rest of the guests. I sometimes wonder if Sanjeewa regrets dedicating his life to hotel work. All that trouble that has to be taken to satisfy the whims of demanding visitors. Although he's been very successful at the job, his undoubted abilities would have enabled him to do many other things. Perhaps he should make a change of career.'

He raised his hands and held them apart, palms facing. 'I

can see it now: an office door with "Sanjeewa Gunesekera, Private Detective", written on a glass panel in big, bold letters.'

Jane pulled a face. 'I'm fond of Sanjeewa but I hope you're not suggesting he permanently supplants me when there's a case to be solved.'

He grinned. 'As if I would. This time is an exception.'

'I'm glad to hear it. Anyway,' she added, 'I very much doubt his wife would agree to his making a change. She dresses so elegantly, and I've always had the impression that she's rather fond of the little luxuries that being married to the manager of a top-class hotel enable her to enjoy. And who can blame her?'

It was de Silva's turn to make a face. 'I hope there are also a few advantages to being a policeman's wife.'

Jane laughed. 'Of course. I didn't mean to imply there weren't. How else would I be able to indulge my love of mysteries?' She drew her wrap tighter around her shoulders. 'I think it's time I went inside. It's beginning to feel a little chilly out here. Are you coming?'

'In a minute.' He raised his glass. 'I'll finish this first.'

Billy trotted in behind Jane, but Bella remained on his lap. His thoughts returned to the three men: Ashok, Raj, and Salman. He still found it hard to believe that Ashok had the ruthless streak he would need to murder Dev, even if he was the obstacle in the way of Ashok's relationship with Layla. Raj was a different kettle of fish. He seemed a more volatile character, and if Anne Collins was right about the bitter resentment he felt for his stepfather, it might be enough to drive him to murder. Salman was the enigma. De Silva cast his mind back to the times he'd seen him: first on the terrace and then by the lake that evening he and Jane had been down there. On both occasions, Salman had seemed unhappy and withdrawn. Had Dev's bullying cut him to the quick and made him view murder as the only escape? It remained to be seen whether he had an alibi, but what about the means to commit the crime? How would he have got into Anne Collins' room? Or had he obtained the digitoxin in some other way? He sighed. Perhaps inspiration would come with the morning.

He drank the last of his whisky and stood up, tucking Bella under one arm. She gave a little mew of protest and wriggled out of his grasp then vanished into the bungalow with a whisk of her tail. He followed and when he'd made sure all the doors were locked up for the night, went to the bedroom.

'Have you found the answer yet?' asked Jane, looking at him over the top of her mystery novel.

'Sadly not, and increasingly I fear we may be on borrowed time. The Khans have to leave Nuala eventually.'

'Hopefully not too soon.'

By the time he'd washed and changed into his pyjamas, Jane had finished reading. 'Try not to worry,' she said. 'Your cases always have a way of working out.'

De Silva sighed. 'I'd like to believe that you're right.' He pointed to the book on her bedside table. 'But unfortunately reality isn't always as obliging as fiction.' He climbed into bed and turned off the bedside lamp. But as he drifted off to sleep, a scenario that he hadn't considered before came into his mind. Was Salman missing because he'd not only murdered his stepfather but also killed himself?

CHAPTER 21

At the station the next morning, de Silva explained to Prasanna and Nadar how his visit to the Faulkners' plantation and his subsequent investigations had cast doubt on Raj's alibi.

'And well done for getting the information about him and Nurse Collins. She's admitted that she made up the story about the maintenance man. She doesn't know if Raj took the digitoxin, but she was afraid he might have done as he still had a key to her room. She was trying to protect him.'

He went on to tell them about the strange goings on at the Residence. 'It seems that the two of you may have to go up there and investigate.'

'Right now, sir?' asked Prasanna, looking surprised.

'No, I'm waiting for Archie's say-so. Anyway, searching for Salman Khan who's still not turned up takes precedence.' He produced the photograph Jane had found and pointed to it. 'Here's the man you're after. We'll need copies of this for ourselves and to distribute around all the regional police forces. Work out the number then one of you go to the print shop and order them.'

Luckily neither of them had set off when Sanjeewa called. 'I've good news for you,' he said. 'Salman's come back. He collected his key from reception and went upstairs. I thought of trying to detain him somehow whilst I called you, but then I decided it would look suspicious, so I sent a couple of our chambermaids up with instructions to look busy at the entrance to the corridor where his room's situated. I told them to let me know immediately if he comes out.'

'If ever you'd like a permanent role in the police force…'

Sanjeewa laughed. 'It's tempting.'

'I'll be with you as soon as possible.'

De Silva went out to the public room. 'We have a change of plan. Salman's turned up.'

'Shall we go to the Residence instead?' asked Prasanna.

'Let me confirm with Archie first. I'll telephone him later. Also, tomorrow would be better. Probably just before dawn. If it's a wild animal causing the trouble, dawn is the most likely time it will emerge from wherever it hides.'

The two young officers looked doubtful.

'If you're worried about protection, you can take a couple of stout sticks with you, but I'm not suggesting you approach this interloper. Just find out what we're dealing with. Oh, and I know it'll be cold at that time of day,' he added. 'You may allow yourselves some latitude in the matter of uniform.'

'Shall we stay here for now?' asked Prasanna.

De Silva thought for a moment. 'No, you'd better come to the Crown with me. I might need you.'

* * *

They went out to the Morris, and de Silva covered the distance to the Crown as fast as the usual congestion of ox carts, handcarts, donkeys, and pedestrians in the streets of Nuala allowed. When they arrived, he told Prasanna and Nadar to stay with the Morris and went up the stairs to the hotel entrance. Apprehension gripped him. He hoped that Salman hadn't yet gone to visit Sunita and Layla. An interview with them present was bound to be much more awkward than one with only himself and Salman. If he was with them and had to be called away, it was also likely to lead to problems. The last thing de Silva wanted to do at the moment was alarm them.

Luckily, when Sanjeewa came out to meet him and they went up together to the corridor where Salman's room was situated, the chambermaids confirmed that he was still inside.

'Well, I'd better get on with questioning him,' said de Silva. 'My constable and my sergeant are outside with the car. Would you send someone down to fetch them? I'd like them here in case he tries to make a run for it.'

Sanjeewa nodded and turned to one of the chambermaids. 'See to it, please.'

The woman waggled her head. 'Yes, sahib.'

With Prasanna and Nadar in position, de Silva knocked on Salman's door and waited. It was strange how loud silence seemed sometimes. Behind him, Sanjeewa shifted his weight from one foot to the other and softly cleared his throat. 'We're on the second floor,' he whispered. 'I can't see how he can have left the room. The climb would be very dangerous, and he'd be likely to be seen.'

Either he was pretending not to be there, thought de Silva, or there was a more sinister explanation. He sensed Sanjeewa's anxiety. Another death in the hotel would be the last thing he wanted. 'Do you think we should go in anyway?' Sanjeewa asked. 'I have a key.'

De Silva raised a hand and knocked again. 'Mr Khan, I know you're in there. I'm Inspector de Silva of the Nuala police. I need to speak to you. Open the door, please.'

For a moment, the silence persisted, then there were footsteps. The door opened to reveal Salman. 'Come in,' he said tersely, then turned and walked away down the short passage that led past the bathroom into the bedroom. De Silva and Sanjeewa followed him.

The bedroom was furnished with a high bed with a carved mahogany headboard and a crimson satin counterpane. A large wardrobe, a chest of drawers, and the bedside tables were made of the same wood. A three-branched bronze chandelier hung from the centre of the ceiling. Salman went to the window then turned back to face them. Even in the dim light coming through the net curtains, de Silva saw that his eyes were red-rimmed. His clothes looked as if he'd slept in them, and his hair was uncombed. There was a smell of alcohol. Was he already aware Dev was dead, even if he hadn't killed him? Or was something else going on?

'What do you want?' Salman asked abruptly.

'I have some questions for you regarding your stepfather. It's my sad duty to tell you that he's dead. I understand that on the day he died, you left the hotel in the morning. I'd like to know where you've been.'

A look of shock came over Salman's face. Was it feigned or genuine?

'How can he be dead? There was nothing wrong with him when I left.'

'I'll come to that. First, I'd like you to tell me where you've been.'

'I've been staying in town. I needed to get away and have some time by myself.'

'Where did you stay?'

'I forget the place's name.'

'Really? That's very convenient.'

Salman glowered at him.

'Was anyone with you?'

Salman hesitated for a fraction of a second then shook his head. 'No, I was on my own.'

'Why did you stay away from the hotel for so long?'

The question hung in the air like the note of tuning fork.

148

'I told you, I needed time on my own.'

'Mr Khan, information has come to light that indicates that your stepfather's death wasn't due to natural causes. We suspect that the murderer stole some digitoxin from Nurse Collins' room with the intention of giving your stepfather an overdose. A needle mark was found on his body, but Nurse Collins confirms she always gave him his medicine by mouth. I've been told that you and your stepfather weren't on good terms. If you've no one to vouch for your movements at the time of his death, you are, inevitably, a prime suspect. Do you want to change or add to anything you've told me?'

The expression on Salman's face slowly turned from one of defiance to hopelessness then he sank to the floor, his arms clasping his knees to his chest and his head bowed.

'I'm not a murderer,' he said dully. 'You're right that Dev and I didn't get on, but I didn't kill him. I've never even touched him in anger.'

'I've only your word for that, Mr Khan. I'm afraid you leave me no choice. I'm placing you under arrest.'

CHAPTER 22

'Hello, dear, I didn't expect to see you until this evening. Have you had lunch?'

'Not yet, and I'm as hungry as a donkey.'

'A horse, Shanti.'

Jane got up from the little bureau where she had been sitting writing up her household accounts and went to the bellpull by the drawing room door.

'I'm sure cook can find something nice for you. I wasn't hungry at lunchtime and I'm still not. Florence held a meeting of the committee that's organising the summer fête this morning. The Residence's cook sent out so many delicious snacks to keep us going that I couldn't eat another mouthful.'

De Silva remembered the snacks that were always on offer when he attended Florence's parties at the Residence. 'I'm most envious.' He also remembered he needed to speak to Archie about sending Prasanna and Nadar.

Their servant Delisha answered the bell and went off to the kitchen to speak to the cook. 'Let's sit on the verandah whilst we wait, shall we,' said Jane. 'You can tell me about your morning. Have there been any developments?'

'There certainly have,' he said as they went outside. 'We didn't need that photograph in the end. Sanjeewa telephoned from the hotel to tell me that Salman Khan had returned. I went straight up there to interview him. He has no alibi for the time when Dev was killed and refused to explain why he left the hotel that day and what he's been doing all the time he's been away. I've placed him under arrest and he's at the station with Prasanna and Nadar in charge. He seems a stubborn fellow. If I'm right about his being guilty, I think it's going to be hard work to get a confession out of him.'

'Do you think Anne Collins helped him?' asked Jane with a frown.

'That's not so clear. I suppose she could be lying about her affair with Raj and his having a spare key to her room. It might really be Salman she's involved with. But what Prasanna heard from some of the actors at the party after the devil dancing scene was filmed bears out that her affair was with Raj.'

'Maybe Salman obtained the digitoxin from another source. Why don't you ask David Hebden how easy that would be?'

'Good idea. I'll try to catch him at his surgery now.'

David Hebden was available. De Silva soon had the answer to his enquiry and briefly answered Hebden's own questions about what had been happening with the case.

'Digitoxin can't be bought over the counter,' he said when he returned to Jane. 'One would need a doctor's prescription. Salman's a young man. He's much slighter than his brother and doesn't carry himself with the same air of confidence, but he looks fit enough. I may be wrong, but if he didn't steal the medicine from Anne Collins, I doubt he persuaded a doctor he needed it.'

'What if he and his brother are in this together?'

'That's another possibility that has to be considered. Raj stealing the medicine from Anne Collins' room but Salman using it.'

'Will you arrest Raj too?'

De Silva frowned. 'I have his connection with Anne

Collins, and the doubt hanging over his alibi, but no, I think I'll hold back for the moment. If luck is on my side, he may give himself away, or I may get a confession out of Salman.'

Lunch arrived and de Silva tucked into vegetable curry and lime pickle served with a plentiful helping of rice.

'What about rest of the Khan family?' asked Jane as he ate. 'When will you tell them Salman's been arrested?'

De Silva sighed. 'I ought not to leave it much longer. With the possible exception of Raj and Ashok if either of them is guilty, they still believe Dev died of heart failure. Unfortunately, I can't let them go on believing that for ever.'

He spooned some more lime pickle onto his rice. 'I think it's high time I went to see Archie. He doesn't know about the latest developments, and if he wants our help, it will also be an opportunity to arrange for Prasanna and Nadar to go up to the Residence to scout around for this interloper who's causing trouble.'

He paused for a moment. 'On second thoughts, one of them will need to stay at the station to keep an eye on Salman. I suppose I ought to make this search at the Residence with the other. Two sets of eyes are better than one, and it would be wrong to expect my officers to do something I'm not prepared to do myself.'

'Then please be careful,' said Jane with a worried frown.

'Of course I will.' He pushed his plate away. 'An excellent meal, I feel like a new man. Time to tackle Archie. I'll just make a quick call to be sure he's at the Residence this afternoon and will see me.'

* * *

The afternoon sun beat down on the Residence's white façade. The flowers in the beds beneath the windows drooped. The hot, dry month of April was always an unforgiving one. As he walked across the gravel from where he'd parked the Morris to the entrance steps, de Silva reflected briefly that next month's rains would be a blessed relief, despite the inconveniences of the monsoon season.

He rang the bell, and the servant who answered the door smiled in recognition. A few months previously, de Silva had helped his family when they had been having difficulties with an unpleasant neighbour.

'Good afternoon, sahib.'

'Good afternoon to you too, Arvindra. I hope you've had no more trouble with your neighbour.'

'None, thanks to you, sahib.'

'Good. Sahib Clutterbuck's expecting me. Is he in his study?'

Arvindra grinned. 'He is expecting you, sahib, but he's not in his study. He is engaged in important work in the garden.'

'Really?' De Silva had never put Archie down as a gardener. 'Where will I find him?'

'On the lawn beside the tennis courts.'

'Thank you, I'll go and find him.'

As he came around the corner of the hedge that screened the tennis court area from the rest of the garden, de Silva heard a tapping sound. Golf club in hand, and dressed in baggy, dun-coloured trousers with a sleeveless jumper knitted in a Fair Isle pattern over his shirt, Archie was watching his golf ball roll slowly over the parched turf towards a small red flag that stuck up from the ground. The ball went wide, lost momentum, and came to rest a foot away from the flag. Grimacing, Archie walked over and scooped it up then put it in one of his trouser pockets.

'Good afternoon, sir!'

His boss turned and raised a hand in greeting. 'Ah, de Silva. I thought we'd talk out here. I just wanted to get in a bit of practice. Take my mind off things, y'know. Let's take a pew over there.' He pointed to a bench in the shade of a palm tree. Darcy had wedged himself firmly underneath it in a position that didn't look very comfortable. 'It's the first time in days I've persuaded the old chap to come so far from the house,' said Archie.

At the bench, Archie rested his club against the seat and removed his hat. His hair was plastered to his head and his cheeks were redder than usual. His forehead glistened. He pulled a handkerchief from his pocket and proceeded to mop his face. 'I ought to know better than to be outdoors at this time of day,' he observed.

De Silva thought, but didn't say, that if Archie would adopt local dress rather than clothing better suited to the British climate he would be more comfortable, but his attitude wasn't unusual. Not many Britishers took a particularly practical approach to Ceylon's climate.

'So, what news have you got for me?'

'Salman Khan has been found.'

'Good. And what does he have to say for himself?'

Archie listened whilst de Silva explained everything that had been happening since their last meeting.

'I take your point about Raj Khan's alibi,' said Archie at last, 'but for my money, you're on the right track with Salman.' He scratched his chin. 'Admittedly, Raj could have been his accomplice and used the key the nurse gave him to get hold of the medicine.'

He paused for a moment before continuing. 'I suggest we leave Ashok Mehta out of it for the moment, despite the conversation you overheard.'

Darcy whined and shifted in his cramped quarters. Archie bent down to pat him. 'His words could be interpreted in more ways than one and surely someone would have seen him leaving the hotel. All the same, no harm in keeping an eye on him. Can't be too careful. When do you plan to question Salman again?'

'I propose to leave it until tomorrow now.'

'Let him stew, eh? Not a bad idea. Give time for the gravity of his situation to sink in.'

'Of course if he continues to deny murdering Dev, he may change his mind and want to have a lawyer present, although at the moment he says he doesn't.'

'Hmm, that seems rather unusual.' Archie cleared his throat. 'It's a relief that the ladies have a solid alibi. Murder's a nasty business at the best of times, but I've always found it particularly repugnant when a lady's the villain.'

He jabbed the putter at the short grass. 'Well, if we're to tell the family that Salman's been arrested for the murder of his stepfather, we'd better get on with it. You can arrange the meeting with Gunesekera but I suggest you let me do the talking. That will leave you free to observe how they react. Raj in particular.' He winced as he got to his feet, putting some of his weight on the golf club. 'This damned heat. It tickles up the old aches and pains, I can tell you. You're lucky not to suffer, de Silva.'

'Indeed I am, sir.'

'Although we both carry a bit more weight than we should.' Archie smiled ruefully. 'As Mrs Clutterbuck never fails to remind me.'

De Silva smiled back. 'My wife also.'

'Ah well, the good things in life are there to be enjoyed, eh? *Let me have men about me that are fat,*' he suddenly declaimed. '*Sleek-headed men and such as sleep at night. Cassius has a lean and hungry look. He thinks too much. Such men are dangerous.*' He paused. 'Julius Caesar. Acted the part at school. Always managed to put ideas in a nutshell, did old Will Shakespeare. Well, no time to dawdle. Anything else before we get on with the job in hand?'

'Only that I was wondering if you'd like any help trying to find this unwelcome interloper.'

'Ah, yes. I'd forgotten about your offer. Exactly what do you have in mind?'

De Silva explained about his plan for a dawn stakeout.

'It can't do any harm,' said Archie after a few moments' thought. 'I'd be grateful if you'd arrange it.' Aches and pains apparently forgotten, he shouldered his club and strode off towards the Residence, Darcy slinking at his heels. Following them, de Silva smiled inwardly at the picture of his boss dressed in Roman toga, sandals, and laurel wreath that rose in his mind. There were times when Archie surprised him.

CHAPTER 23

As they stood at the door to Sunita's suite waiting to be admitted, de Silva cast a sideways glance at Archie. His boss looked composed, but did his outward demeanour truly reflect his inward state? De Silva hoped he didn't look uncomfortable himself. Hard as he tried, he was unable to ignore his churning stomach. Unless what they were about to say came as no surprise to the people in the room, it was going to increase what must already be deep distress. The duty of telling a victim's family that their relation had been murdered was one of the most difficult tasks his job required him to do.

'Chin up,' muttered Archie. 'Don't forget what we agreed.'

There was a slight note of uncertainty in his voice. De Silva derived a modicum of comfort from the thought that he might not be the only one who felt apprehensive.

The door opened to reveal Raj Khan. He stood aside to let them into a large drawing room. The walls were painted a deep rose-red and curtains in the same shade hung at the tall windows, tied back with gold tasselled cords. More gold picked out the cornices and the dado rail running around the room. The floor was made of highly polished dark wood as was the furniture. De Silva found the effect rather overpowering, but it certainly had dramatic impact. Presumably, that appealed to Sunita Khan. Several ceiling fans rotated gently, making the air pleasantly cool.

Sunita reclined on a chaise longue upholstered in gold damask. On a nearby chair sat Layla, her back ramrod straight, her knees pressed tightly together, and her hands clasped in her lap. Her whole body radiated tension and anxiety. De Silva wondered if it was because she already knew why he and Archie had come. Ashok stood behind her chair, one hand on her shoulder. He looked much calmer. No one invited Archie and de Silva to take a seat. It was Raj who spoke first.

'What's this about?' he asked sharply.

De Silva only half listened as Archie explained why they'd come. He was too busy watching the faces in the room. The emotions he detected ranged from sorrow to anger. What seemed to be genuine shock and sorrow on Layla's part – perhaps she hadn't known what to expect after all – and anger on Raj's.

'This is nonsense!' he burst out after a few moments, interrupting Archie who had just explained that Dev appeared to have died of an overdose of digitoxin. 'I can't explain what that syringe was doing near my stepfather's body, but if you're suggesting my brother killed him, it's preposterous. My stepfather has rubbed plenty of people up the wrong way over the years. Salman doesn't have a violent bone in his body.'

'Raj,' Ashok murmured, 'hear him out.'

Raj rounded on him. 'Why should I when this is patently a load of rubbish?' he asked contemptuously. His dark eyes flashed.

Sunita raised a hand. She was dry-eyed, but de Silva saw that she trembled. 'Be quiet, Raj. Like you, I believe there's been a mistake, but anger won't help.'

A peevish expression came across Raj's face. He grumbled but to de Silva's surprise, subsided into silence. Sunita turned to Archie. 'We'll fight to prove my stepson's innocence,' she said quietly. 'Have no doubt about that.'

'Your loyalty does you credit, ma'am, but I'm afraid that for the moment, he must stay under arrest.'

* * *

'Well, what's your opinion now?' asked Archie when after further exchanges, most of them heated, they'd taken their leave and were on their way back to the lobby.

'I had the impression that the news came as a surprise to all of them.'

'I thought so too. It leaves us where we were before: with Salman as our man. We'll have to wait and see what the Khans' next move will be. Interesting that they didn't demand to see Salman, but I expect they will when they've got over the initial shock. I wonder if they'll want to use Bombay lawyers to defend him.'

They had reached the lobby. It was quiet with an air of late afternoon torpor lying over it. Nevertheless, Archie lowered his voice. 'If despite what Salman told you about not wanting a lawyer, the family persuade him to change his mind, it may cause a significant delay whilst one's found, but there's nothing we can do about it.'

They descended the steps to the drive. After the coolness of Sunita's suite and the lobby, the heat of the sun made de Silva reach to loosen his collar. Archie expelled a puff of air. 'Well, I'll be off back to the Residence. Keep me informed if there are any developments.'

'Of course.'

* * *

De Silva arrived home to find Jane on the verandah having tea. 'You look weary, dear,' she said.

He sat down in his chair with a sigh of relief. 'I must admit I am.'

161

She reached for the little bell on the table next to her and rang it. 'Let me ask one of the servants to bring you some tea then you can tell me what's been going on.'

'A fresh pot of tea and a cup for the sahib, please,' she said when their servant Leela appeared.

'Yes, memsahib.'

'Archie and I've spoken to the family now,' said de Silva when Leela had gone. 'They know that Salman has been arrested.'

Jane sighed. 'It must have been a difficult conversation. To learn that a loved one's dead and then that they were murdered, apparently by a member of one's own family, is a triple blow.'

'Yes. Dev's daughter Layla was very distressed. I think Sunita, his widow, was too, but she behaved in a most dignified manner. It was quite surprising for a lady who has a reputation for being volatile.'

'What about Salman's brother Raj?'

'If the fact that Dev was murdered rather than dying from natural causes didn't come as a surprise to him, he gave a very convincing performance. He was furious that his brother has been arrested. He kept insisting that Salman would never kill anyone. That if Dev had been murdered, we had the wrong man.'

'It says something for his character that he's loyal to his brother. Did he come up with a suggestion as to who might have done it?'

De Silva shook his head.

'How did Ashok react?'

'He seemed calm. Very concerned to lower the temperature of the meeting and comfort the ladies, particularly Layla. All of them denied knowing where Salman was before he returned to the hotel this morning. I'm afraid it's hard to come to any conclusion other than that he murdered Dev.'

'What a terrible way for things to work out,' said Jane with a shiver. 'I know murder's a dreadful crime, but for such a young man to lose his life when more sympathy and understanding from his stepfather might have prevented the tragedy—'

'You have a kind heart, my love, but the law must take its course.'

They fell silent as Leela returned with the tea. Jane poured him out a cup and de Silva raised it to his lips, inhaled the reviving aroma and took a sip. 'Ah, that's good.'

'You still need to establish how Salman obtained the digitoxin, is that right?'

'Yes, I do. Raj didn't react when Archie suggested it might have been stolen from Anne Collins' room. That might be because he's hiding that he took it, but it could merely be that he doesn't want to give away the fact that he has a key because of their affair. I'll have to get him on his own and question him again, but I suspect he's a tough customer. Particularly if he's trying to protect his brother.'

CHAPTER 24

'How's our prisoner been?' asked de Silva when he returned to the station.

'No trouble, sir,' said Prasanna with a shrug. 'In fact, he doesn't say a word. Nadar fetched some food from the bazaar for him a while ago, but he's not touched it, although most people would be hungry by now and he doesn't look as if he's had a decent meal in days.'

'It's as if he's in a world of his own,' added Nadar.

De Silva thought of the lines Archie had quoted from Shakespeare's play: *Cassius has a lean and hungry look. He thinks too much: such men are dangerous.* Were they an apt description of Salman?

'Well, all one can do is try. I hope it's going to be easier to get answers out of him than it is to get food in. Now, about this search at the Residence tomorrow morning. One of you'll need to stay here to keep an eye on our prisoner. I'll go up with the other one.'

Nadar and Prasanna glanced at each other. 'Shall I stay with the prisoner, sir?' asked Prasanna.

'If you like. Then you can come with me, Nadar. I suggest we meet at the Residence at five.'

'I'll be there, sir.'

'You can both take a couple of hours off now if you wish. I'll take charge of the prisoner.'

He watched through the window as Prasanna and Nadar

unchained their bicycles and pedalled away in the direction of the bazaar. He wondered if they would go home for a while. He reflected that neither of them had mentioned the matter of the pay rise again. He hoped they weren't disappointed at the lack of progress. He doubted Prasanna's wife Kuveni would be making a fuss, but he suspected that Nadar's might be complaining at him.

He turned away from the window. Despite what he'd said to Archie about letting Salman sweat, he might pay him a visit.

The drab walls of the corridor that led to the cells echoed de Silva's footsteps. The air grew stuffier, and the light dimmed. He stopped outside the first of the two cells that the station possessed, and regarded Salman. The young man lay on his back on the narrow bed, his eyes closed. The bowl of food Nadar had brought was on the floor beside him. It had no doubt been perfectly edible once, but now it looked congealed and unappetising. The sickly light falling from the window high in the wall opposite the bars did nothing to relieve the bleakness of the scene.

Salman opened his eyes and turned his head to look at de Silva. 'Have you come to tell me I can go?'

'Until you have an alibi for the time of your stepfather's death, you know I'm unable to do that. I urge you to think very carefully, Mr Khan. We're not playing a game. Your situation is one of great peril. Your freedom, even your life is at stake. If you can offer anything in your defence, you should do so. As you're aware, if you wish it, you have the right to have a lawyer present whilst you are questioned.'

A fleeting glimpse of uncertainty came into the young man's eyes, then it was gone. 'You have my word that I didn't kill my stepfather,' he said wearily. 'But I've nothing else to say. And I don't want a lawyer.'

Before he turned his face to the wall, de Silva saw the sheen of tears in his eyes and felt a stab of pity mixed with irritation. He wasn't sure why he had the feeling that the young man was hiding something. If it was information he could use in his defence, why would he do that? There was a disarming quality to him. He seemed very different to his brother, and all the better for lacking Raj's quick temper and air of entitlement. If a clever barrister could bring out that quality in court, it was just possible that a jury might be swayed in his favour and believe his denial, but it would be unfair to raise his hopes.

'I'm afraid your word is not enough,' he said quietly. 'I'll come back later. Perhaps when you've had time to reflect, you'll have something more to tell me.'

'No!' The sharpness of Salman's tone took de Silva aback. 'I've nothing more to say,' he added in a calmer voice. De Silva sighed. Salman wasn't the only reluctant prisoner he'd had to deal with in the course of his career, but he had a nasty feeling that he was going to be one of the harder ones to persuade to talk. And why was he so insistent that he didn't want a lawyer?

* * *

When Prasanna and Nadar returned, de Silva decided to take another look around at the Crown. He wasn't sure what he was looking for, but he couldn't shake off the feeling that there was something he'd missed. He was crossing the lobby when he saw Sanjeewa coming to greet him.

'Nothing to report since you left earlier,' he said. 'The family and Ashok are all in their rooms. How's Salman getting on?'

'Not in good shape, I'm afraid. Hardly surprising in the circumstances. He denies he was responsible, but without an alibi he'll need a great deal of luck to escape being convicted, and he refuses to tell me where he was at the time of his stepfather's death or since.'

Sanjeewa looked at him closely. 'Do I detect you have doubts about his guilt?'

De Silva pulled a face. 'Logic tells me that there's no room for that, but there's something about him – a vulnerability that makes it hard to believe he's a killer.' He shrugged. 'Perhaps I'm letting sentiment rule my head.'

'Probably unwise in your line of work,' said Sanjeewa. 'But I know what you mean. From the little contact I've had with him since the Khan family has been staying here, I've found him a far more sympathetic character than his stepfather or his brother.'

'I'd like to take another look around Anne Collins' room. I'm sure Prasanna and Nadar did a good job, but—'

'Sometimes small details can be missed?'

'Exactly.'

'Why don't I come with you?'

'Very well.'

In Anne Collins' room, a light dusting of powder from Prasanna's and Nadar's search for fingerprints dulled the shine on the polished surfaces. In places, more powder sprinkled the carpet like a featherlight fall of snow.

'As you see,' said Sanjeewa, 'nothing's been touched. But if after this you're satisfied there's nothing left to find, I'd like to tell housekeeping the room can be cleaned and made available for other guests. Unless you think Anne Collins can come back, of course.'

'She's better off where she is,' said de Silva, breaking off from surveying the room. 'By all means prepare the room for another guest.'

'Do you still want me to keep Dev's suite out of bounds?'

'Yes.'

Sanjeewa ran a finger over one of the bedside tables, leaving a trail in the fine dust. He held the finger up for inspection. 'Your lads certainly did a thorough job.'

'I should hope so.'

'Well, I'll leave you to spin your theories.'

'I'm not sure I have any,' said de Silva ruefully. 'At least none that will prove Salman innocent.'

Sanjeewa smiled. 'If he is, the truth will out somehow.'

'I hope you're right.'

'I'll be in my office if you want to see me when you're done.' Sanjeewa walked towards the door and as he did so, paused to retrieve something from the rug by the bed. When he straightened up again, there were two hairpins in his hand.

'These shouldn't be on the floor.' He put them on top of the chest of drawers. 'The chambermaids are sure to see them there and clear them away.'

The door closed behind him, and de Silva went back to surveying the room. He couldn't fault the work Prasanna and Nadar had done. They'd certainty used enough powder. They'd checked the cupboard where the electricity controls were situated too. If Raj had stolen the digitoxin to give to his brother, or to use on his stepfather himself, he wasn't going to find proof of it here.

He went to the window and looked out. They were on the third floor facing the back of the hotel. It was a quiet road and someone climbing up to the window was unlikely to be noticed, but it would be a difficult climb. If not by Raj using Anne Collins' key, how had the digitoxin been obtained? Maybe before the Khans left Bombay from a doctor who didn't ask too many questions?

Downstairs, the lobby was busy with guests returning from their afternoon activities. De Silva was weaving his way through the crowd towards the door to the private area of the hotel and Sanjeewa's office when he saw his friend coming towards him. It was obvious he was in a hurry.

'A problem?'

Sanjeewa rolled his eyes. 'When isn't there? But it will have to wait if there's something urgent that you'd like to discuss.'

'No, nothing at the moment. I'll be off and leave you to your work.'

Back at the police station, Prasanna and Nadar were in the public room.

'Anything to report?' asked de Silva.

Prasanna shook his head. 'No, sir, the prisoner still hasn't said a word. And the new food we fetched hasn't been touched.'

De Silva sighed. 'Well, you've tried. You may go home for a few hours, Prasanna, then come back and take over from Nadar. Nadar, I'll see you at the Residence in the morning as we arranged.'

CHAPTER 25

As de Silva drove onto the sweep of gravel in front of the Residence just before five o'clock the following morning, the Morris's headlights picked out the figure of Nadar chaining up his bicycle. He straightened up and came over to the car.

'Good morning, sir.' He'd taken de Silva at his word and his hands were encased in woollen gloves. He also wore a knitted hat pulled well down over his ears and a voluminous burnt-orange shawl over his jacket.

'It is my wife's,' he said apologetically.

'Never mind, this isn't a fashion parade. Now, where shall we start?'

'There's a small wood beyond the lake.'

De Silva frowned. 'That's rather a long way from the house, isn't it?'

'I think it will be best, sir.'

As they walked through the formal gardens, heading for the lake, de Silva cast curious glances at Nadar. The young man seemed very sure of where he was going.

'What makes you so certain this is the best place to start?' he asked eventually.

Nadar grinned. 'I spoke with some of the garden staff after you mentioned the problem. They gave me some useful information.'

De Silva was puzzled. 'Then why haven't they dealt with this intruder themselves?'

'They are afraid, sir.'

De Silva felt a twinge of alarm. What was this inter-loper? A hungry leopard? An enraged elephant? But what would either of those want with spectacles and teaspoons?

'Sergeant Prasanna is also afraid,' Nadar went on with a touch of smugness in his voice. 'That is why he preferred to guard the prisoner.'

De Silva was about to remark that he might have made a wise choice when Nadar chuckled. 'He was attacked by an angry peacock when he was a little boy.'

'A peacock?'

'Yes, sir. That is what has been stealing shiny things and alarming Sahib and Memsahib Clutterbuck's pets.'

De Silva started to laugh then suddenly sobered. A peck from an angry peacock might be most unpleasant. Undeniably, they were some of the most beautiful birds in existence, but they also had a reputation for being aggressive.

They had reached the lake where a thin veil of mist hung over the surface. At the water margin, a few bulrushes poked through it. As he followed Nadar around to the far side, de Silva smelled damp vegetation.

There was a thin line of red on the eastern horizon and the sky was growing lighter, but it was still quite dark under the tree canopy in the small wood. De Silva waited a moment for his eyes to adjust. From what he could see, the wood was going to be easier to navigate than the depths of the jungle, but there were still tree roots to step over and low-hanging branches to avoid, to say nothing of being on the alert for snakes.

A short walk brought them to a clearing. 'There's the nest, sir,' said Nadar, pointing to a shallow depression scraped out at the edge of some undergrowth. The morning light had penetrated the trees now, and de Silva saw something glint in the bare soil. It looked suspiciously like a teaspoon, and was that a pair of spectacles nearby? He was about to go closer for a better look when there was a strange sound behind him. It was like the zizzing noise Jane's sewing machine made when she was speedily sewing a straight seam.

He swung round and saw the peacock. It was no more than ten feet away from them, its tail feathers raised in a shining green hemisphere studded with chestnut and royal-blue oculi. As it shimmied from one foot to the other, it looked like an exotic dancer lost in the rhythm of music no one else could hear. Its plumed head jerked from side to side and its beady eyes added to the air of malevolence that it exuded. Suddenly, it paused, dipped its tail feathers, and made a sally in their direction. Involuntarily, de Silva took a step back and nearly lost his balance, but Nadar stood firm.

'He won't hurt us, sir.'

De Silva wasn't sure how his constable worked that out, but he was right. The bird stopped a few feet away and lowered its tail feathers. De Silva noticed that Nadar had produced a small brown-paper bag. It appeared to be moving of its own accord. He opened it wide and tossed the contents onto the ground a little to one side of where the peacock was standing. Immediately, the ground became a writhing mass of crickets, spiders, ants, and worms. The peacock began to peck hungrily at them.

'Phew!' De Silva mopped his brow then remembered that it didn't do to let his constable know he'd been unnerved, although a glance at Nadar told him it was a bit late for that.

'I'm sorry, sir. It was unwise of me to let you stand so close to the nest. This bird has a bit of a temper. I think it might be because he's lost his mate. Maybe he's been collecting things from the garden to make up for the fact that there will be no eggs in the nest.'

The peacock had made short work of Nadar's feast and was watching them in a way de Silva didn't like. 'Have you anything else to give him?' he asked.

'Some nice pieces of fig.' Nadar produced a smaller bag and threw the contents to the bird. De Silva smelled the musky sweetness of the fig's juicy pink flesh. It seemed a shame to waste it on a bird, but at least it was saving them from being pecked.

'Well, where do we go from here?'

'He'll be sure to attack if we try to take his treasures from the nest. We'll have to capture him and take him to a different place a good way from here.'

De Silva raised an eyebrow. 'As easy as that, eh?'

'Not easy, sir,' said Nadar seriously. 'But I think I can make a cage big enough to entice and trap him in without harming him. Then he can be moved on a cart or a truck.'

'Good.' He looked at his watch. 'It's rather early to disturb the Clutterbucks. I think we can go back to town and have some breakfast in the bazaar. I'll telephone later.'

CHAPTER 26

De Silva had forgotten that young men tend to have large appetites. Breakfast in the bazaar was a lengthier affair than it would have been if he'd only been satisfying his own hunger, but he reflected that Nadar deserved a good feed after his impressive performance with the rogue peacock.

When they finally arrived at the station, Prasanna greeted them from behind the desk in the public room. He wasn't alone. A man dressed in casual but obviously good quality western-style trousers and shirt was sitting in the waiting area. He appeared to be in his late twenties and de Silva had a vague feeling that he recognised him. He went up to the desk.

'All quiet, Prasanna?'

'Yes, sir. But the prisoner still refuses to eat or talk.' Prasanna nodded in the direction of the man sitting on the chair. 'And this gentleman wants to speak with you. He says it's urgent.'

'Well, I'm pleased to say that our errand was fruitful, but I'll explain about that in due course.' De Silva turned to the man. 'You'd better come into my office.'

In his office, he gestured to the chair on the opposite side of the desk from his own. 'Please, take a seat.' He went around the desk and sat down, trying to place where he might have seen this man before. There was definitely something familiar about him. 'Have we already met?' he asked.

'I don't believe so. My name is Bedu, Hari Bedu. I'm the director of the film that was being made by Dev Khan in Nuala.'

De Silva frowned. Wasn't the director supposed to be in Colombo? Still, no doubt all would be revealed. 'What can I do for you, Mr Bedu?'

Hari Bedu didn't answer for a few moments. As de Silva waited for him to speak, it suddenly came to him where he'd seen the director before. Not on the film set, but a few days ago when he'd been eating lunch in the square where the woman was washing clothes by the water tank. Bedu had come out of one of the houses and spoken to her. Money had changed hands.

Bedu still seemed disinclined to speak, so de Silva broke the silence. 'I'm afraid I don't have all day. If there's something I can help you with—'

Bedu found his voice. 'I understand you're holding Salman Khan here and he's accused of his stepfather's murder.'

'Who told you that?'

'Ashok Mehta.'

There was another silence, again broken by de Silva. 'If you have any information that's relevant to the case, sir, I'll be glad to hear it.' He saw that there were beads of sweat on the director's forehead. His expression was a strange mixture of anxiety and defiance.

'Mr Bedu?'

Suddenly, the director leant forward and gripped the edge of the desk. The veins at his temples bulged. 'Yes, I have something to tell you. Salman wasn't the one who murdered his stepfather.'

'And how can you be so sure of that?'

'Because he and I were together for the whole of that day.'

De Silva frowned. So why had Salman refused to give Hari Bedu as his alibi?

Then he remembered how, shortly after Hari had paid the woman in the square, he'd seen another man who'd hesitated on the threshold of the house's front door but had not come out. All at once, it came to him why Salman hadn't given Bedu's name. According to Ashok, all of the film people apart from himself and the Khans had left for Colombo by then. If Salman was the man in the house and Bedu had stayed behind secretly to spend time with him, it indicated there was something between them that they most certainly wouldn't want made public. Another look at Bedu's troubled expression convinced him that he was right.

'I expect you'd like to see Salman,' he said quietly.

'Thank you. I would.'

* * *

After he'd allowed Salman and Hari Bedu some time together then sent the director on his way with a warning not to speak to anyone else for the moment, de Silva closed his office door and sat down at his desk to contemplate the dilemma facing him. In his own Buddhist faith, there was more than one view concerning relationships between grown men. One of them held that if there was love between the men and no harm was done, such relationships were acceptable. The British view was, however, different. The Christian religion firmly outlawed all such unions. They were a crime that was severely punished by the English law. De Silva admired Salman's courage. By hiding that he and Hari had been together on the day of Dev's death, he had been trying to protect his lover, even though it was likely to lead to his paying a terrible price. Equally, Hari Bedu risked everything by coming to vouch for Salman.

De Silva rested his forehead against the palm of his

hand and squeezed his eyes tight shut, massaging his temples with his thumb and forefinger. He was an officer in the British police force, duty bound to abide by their laws, but he wished there was a way to help the two men.

For a moment, confusion fogged his mind, then a ray of hope dispelled some of it. If they were telling the truth that neither of them was responsible for Dev's murder, and he felt it in his bones that they were, it meant that someone else had killed Dev. So, the way to help them was to find out who that person was as soon as possible. If he could do that, their relationship might not need to be made public. But a moment later, his spirits sank again. How was he to find out, let alone quickly? Soon he would have to charge Salman or let him go. And if he followed the latter course, how was he to explain it without landing the lovers in deep trouble?

CHAPTER 27

When he walked into the hall at Sunnybank, the house seemed very quiet until Bella trotted out from the direction of the kitchen to meet him, weaving herself around his legs and purring. He bent down to pick her up. 'Where have your mistress and Billy got to, then?'

The little black cat regarded him with her green eyes and blinked.

'If she's not here,' de Silva said gloomily, 'I'll just have to puzzle over my problem on my own.'

There was the sound of footsteps and one of the servants appeared.

'Good afternoon, Jayasena, is the memsahib out?'

'No, sahib, she's in the garden.'

De Silva brightened. 'Ah, good, I'll go and find her.'

A pair of secateurs in her hand, and her head tilted to one side in contemplation, Jane stood in front of a large fern. He came up behind her and put a hand on her shoulder. She jumped then turned around smiling. 'Sneaking up on me?'

'I'm always suspicious when I see you with a pair of secateurs in your hand.'

'I only need a bit of extra greenery for the church flowers. Anif's already picked those roses we talked about. I thought I'd fetch the greenery myself because I haven't long before I need to leave. I promised to meet Florence and I'm in danger of running late.'

'I'm only teasing.' He brushed a hand over the fern, feeling the leaves ripple under his fingers. 'Take as much as you need. Would you like me to drive you to the church when you're ready?'

'That would be very kind. It will be quicker than sending for a rickshaw.'

Jane snipped off a piece of the fern and placed it in the basket over her arm. 'There, that's enough. Now, you can tell me about your visit to the Residence whilst I get ready.'

On the walk back to the bungalow, he explained about the peacock. 'Who would have thought that Nadar has such a talent for dealing with birds,' she said when he'd finished.

'I'm afraid I didn't put up nearly such a good performance.' De Silva smiled ruefully. 'I hope it wasn't too obvious that the bird unnerved me.'

'Well, what does it matter if it was obvious? Nadar seems to have everything under control. It's good for him to take charge and show what he can do sometimes.'

'I suppose it is.'

She left her basket on the hall table, and de Silva followed her to the bedroom. She sat down at her dressing table and picked up her hairbrush then gave him an inquiring look. 'Have you something else to tell me?'

He made a face. 'I'm afraid so, and not such pleasing news. This murder case has taken an unexpected turn. I thought I'd got the culprit, but now I'm not so sure.'

'But if whatever you've discovered means Salman's in the clear, is that such a bad thing? I feel very sorry for him.'

'Unfortunately, the situation's not as straightforward as that.'

He proceeded to tell her about Hari Bedu's visit to the police station. 'So,' he concluded, 'I need a way to shield them from trouble without going against my duty.'

Jane sighed and shook her head. 'It will be a fine line to tread.'

'Yes, but with my hand on my heart, I can say that they've not actually confessed to anything illegal, and I have no real proof they've committed any crimes. The difficulty arises if anyone wants to know why Salman was so secretive and didn't reveal his alibi straight away. That's why I need to find out quickly who the real culprit is. Then with luck, no one will ask questions about Salman.'

'I see that.' Jane put down her brush and reached for a pretty little bowl decorated with a black and carmine design of Chinese pagodas and cranes. She tucked her hair into a French pleat and began to anchor it in position with hairgrips from the bowl. Finally, she picked up a hand mirror and surveyed her handiwork.

'There, that should do.' She sighed. 'But I really must do something about my grey hairs.'

'Must you? Your hair looks beautiful to me, my love.'

She stood up and gave him a kiss on the cheek. 'Thank you, but I think I ought to. Especially as I like to pin it up. No one makes grips that match. Anyway, that's for another day. I'm sorry to leave you with your problem but I mustn't keep Florence waiting. It wouldn't help to have to explain to her why, would it?'

De Silva sighed. 'No.'

'Anyway, we can talk more on the way.'

But by the time they arrived at the church, they had yet to come up with a plan for finding out who the murderer was and helping Salman and Hari Bedu.

'Do you want me to fetch you later?' he asked.

'There's no need. I'm sure Florence will give me a lift home, but if not, I'll take a rickshaw.'

'Very well, I'll be off to the station then. I'll see you this evening.'

* * *

181

When he left Jane, however, he decided not to go straight to the station after all. He wanted some fresh air, and sometimes getting away from the bustle of Nuala helped him to think, so instead he drove up to the cricket club. He parked the Morris and wandered over to the area where the film crew had been working. Almost all trace of them was gone now. If it hadn't been for Dev Khan's death, the people involved would be nothing more than a chapter in Nuala's history on which the book was firmly closed.

He picked up a splintered piece of wood that lay near his feet. There was a groove at one end of it. He wondered if it was the broken handle of a mallet used for knocking tent pegs into the ground. The head was nowhere to be seen so it must have come loose. Perhaps someone had kept it and fixed in a new handle.

Fixing things: his mind went back to Jane arranging her hair and the grips she used. She always kept them in the bowl on her dressing table, but he'd never thought about them before. It occurred to him that the ones Jane had were similar in colour to the two Sanjeewa had picked up in Anne Collins' room, but she had fair hair. Jane had mentioned one couldn't buy grips that matched with grey hair, but what about Anne Collins' colour? If it was possible, he felt sure that a woman who seemed as conscious of her appearance as she did would have them. He would ask Jane. It probably wasn't significant, but he never liked to leave loose ends.

He walked a little further then returned to the cricket club. The hands on the clubhouse clock showed it was five, and there were no workmen about. The gleam of white paint on the clubhouse railings and the immaculately shaved turf of the cricket square indicated that for now, their job was done. He wished that his was.

He cast his mind back once again to the hairgrips in Anne Collins' room. If Sanjeewa's chambermaids did their job properly, he was sure they would remove anything that guests had left behind after they vacated a room. So, if the grips didn't belong to Collins, whose were they? Was it just that a chambermaid had missed them, or did they prove that someone else had been in the room whilst Collins was still using it and that person wasn't Raj Khan?

An idea began to take shape in his mind. It needed careful examination, but in the circumstances, anything was worth pursuing. He felt a surge of hope. It would be wonderful if he was on the right track at last. It might not have been a waste of time searching Anne Collins' room again, but what about any clues in Dev Khan's suite? He must get over to the Crown straight away. Thank goodness he'd told Sanjeewa the suite was to be kept locked up.

CHAPTER 28

'I wasn't expecting to see you back so soon,' said Sanjeewa when de Silva was shown into his office. 'Has Salman confessed?'

'No, and I'm convinced now that he's innocent.' He paused. 'What I'm about to tell you needs to be kept between ourselves.'

Sanjeewa frowned. 'You sound very mysterious. But of course I'll do as you ask.'

'Thank you.' De Silva proceeded to explain about Salman and Hari Bedu.

'I see what you mean about keeping it to myself,' said Sanjeewa when he'd finished. 'This could spell disaster for them both.'

'I'd like to go up to Dev's suite. It's occurred to me that I've never searched it properly.'

'Is there anything particular that you hope to find?'

'Do you remember telling me about Mrs Patel and how your hairdresser complained that her hair was very difficult to fix?'

Sanjeewa looked puzzled. 'I think so, but what does that have to do with Dev's murder?'

'Remember those hairpins you found on the floor in Anne Collins' room?'

'Yes, but… Oh, I see. You think they might have belonged to Mrs Patel, and she went in there to look for the medicine bottle. That's a bit of a longshot, isn't it, Shanti? We don't even have evidence she had any connection with Dev.'

'I know, but I'm prepared to consider anything. Let's suppose there is a connection. We might find something in Dev's suite that provides the breakthrough we need.'

Sanjeewa stood up. 'Let me get the key.'

Ten minutes later, Sanjeewa unlocked the door to the suite and they both went in. The curtains had only been left partially closed and the temperature in the drawing room was unbearably hot. Sanjeewa hurried to a window and flung it open, but the air barely stirred.

'Where do we start?'

'Why don't you take the bedroom and bathroom and I'll start in here,' said de Silva.

Sanjeewa headed for the bedroom and de Silva began to search, starting with the mahogany bureau in one corner of the room. The drawers were empty, as was the compartment behind its roll-top front. He was about to move on to a small chest of drawers when he noticed a few crumpled pieces of paper in the wastepaper basket beside the desk. He picked them out and took them to the coffee table in front of the sofa. As he moved aside a vase of dead flowers, his nose wrinkled at the smell of the stagnant water it contained. Carefully, he smoothed out the pieces of paper. The first one was a note from Layla and the next, one from Sunita, but the third gave him a little surge of excitement. It was in Hindi rather than English like the other two, so he couldn't read all of it, but he recognised a few words, including the word "money". There was no signature.

Sanjeewa came into the room. 'I'm afraid I'm not having any luck. How are you doing?' He mopped his face with a handkerchief. 'It's damned hot in there, and Dev certainly liked to splash his cologne about. The bathroom smells like a harem.'

De Silva handed him the piece of paper. 'What do you make of that?'

Sanjeewa studied the note for a moment then looked up at him. 'Do you know, you might be on the right track after all. This does look like Mrs Patel's writing. I've a letter of complaint from her in my office. Let's go back and have a look at it.'

* * *

'One can easily find hairgrips that blend in with fair hair,' said Jane when he arrived home later and explained about his find in Anne Collins' room. 'And I agree that if Anne Collins is particular about her appearance, they're what she'd use. But do you really think that a few stray hairpins are so significant? Even with the Crown's high standards, a chambermaid might have been careless for once. The pins may even have dropped from her own hair.'

'I appreciate that, but in the circumstances, I was loath to ignore the smallest of clues.'

Jane looked at him quizzically. 'And where did it lead you?'

He produced the note. 'To this. I found it in Dev Khan's suite. It was crumpled up in a ball and thrown in the waste-paper basket. It's lucky I told Sanjeewa not to let anyone into the suite, or by now it would probably have been in the hotel's incinerator.'

Jane took the note from him and studied it for a moment then handed it back. 'I can't understand a word. What language is it in?'

'Hindi. Luckily, Sanjeewa quite often has Indian guests at the hotel, so he was able to translate.' He held the letter away from him and Jane shook her head. 'It really is time you had reading glasses, dear.'

'I can still manage perfectly well. Now, where was I? It says: *I have the money for you. Meet me this afternoon at the time and place we agreed. Come alone and tell no one.*'

'Who do you think it's from?'

'Sanjeewa has a difficult guest staying at the Crown. Her name's Mrs Patel. Do you remember I told you that on the afternoon that Dev was murdered, his wife and daughter were having their hair done by the hotel's resident hairdresser, thus giving them an alibi? Well, there was an element of luck in that, because the hairdresser had originally been booked by Mrs Patel, but she cancelled at short notice. Sanjeewa said that the hairdresser was pleased because Mrs Patel's a very demanding customer. She also has hair that's difficult to style. Very thick, and even with a lot of hairpins it's difficult to keep it in place.'

Jane looked sceptical. 'And you made the connection with the hairpins on the floor of Anne Collins' room?'

'Yes.'

'I can't see that they amount to convincing evidence that Mrs Patel's involved, dear,' said Jane doubtfully. 'How can you be sure she wrote the note?'

'Sanjeewa has one from her written when she complained about a maid who she accused of breaking an expensive bottle of perfume. He thought he recognised the writing on the note we found as being the same as that on Mrs Patel's letter of complaint. We went to his office to check, and we think it's plausible Mrs Patel wrote this too.'

'But how would she get into the room? We know the story about the maintenance man is false and anyway, wouldn't it be rather difficult for Mrs Patel to disguise herself as a man?' Jane paused. 'I suppose she might pass as a chambermaid, but she'd need to get hold of a set of overalls and a key.'

'That's possible. Or she might have used one of those hairpins of hers to pick the lock. I had a look at it before I left the hotel, and it's not a complicated one. She might be prepared to take the risk of wearing her own clothes if she knew everyone was at dinner. I must ask Sanjeewa if there's been an evening when she hasn't come down.'

'But what would be her motive for wanting Dev dead?'

'Ah, that's where it gets interesting. When I was up at the Crown on the day that Dev knocked the gardener over with his car, Sanjeewa arranged for me to speak privately with him and Ashok to try to sort out the problem. We met in a small lounge off the lobby. Dev was very difficult at first and Ashok suggested I leave the room for a few moments whilst they talked in private. When I returned, Dev was in a more cooperative mood, and in the end, I thought the interview went quite well. But when we parted company and he passed me on the way out of the room, he paused and muttered a strange remark. It stayed in my mind because at the time it unnerved me.'

'What did he say?'

'I think his words were, "I never forget a face". I thought he meant that I'd made an enemy of him, but afterwards, I decided I was being oversensitive. After all, he was leaving Nuala soon. How could he do me any serious harm? But now I look back on it, I wonder if he was talking about Mrs Patel. She and her husband were in the lobby at the time, right in our line of sight, and she was causing a commotion. He could hardly miss her.'

Jane looked thoughtful. 'But what would be the connection between them?'

'I don't know yet, but I've thought of a discreet way that I might find out. I understand from Ashok that Dev's dresser, Naseer, knew Dev when they were boys and worked for him ever since. If there was a connection between Dev and Mrs Patel and she was the person Dev was voicing his thoughts about, Naseer might be able to throw some light on the situation.'

'I agree it's worth a try. Do you know where to find this man Naseer?'

'I hope he's still in Nuala, but I understand he worked exclusively for Dev, so with him no longer around, there'd be nothing for Naseer to do with the film company. Sanjeewa may know where he's got to. Failing that, I'll have to ask Ashok, although I'd prefer not to let him in on my plan for now. I still haven't ruled him out entirely, and I'd rather no one got wind of the fact that Salman has an alibi after all. If it turns out I'm on the right track with Mrs Patel, it will be much easier to gloss over letting Salman go.'

'That's true. Does Mrs Patel have a husband? Do you think he's involved?'

'He seems a very meek man. Sanjeewa says she's always the one who does the talking, but I suppose I ought not to discount the possibility that he could be a party to the crime.'

CHAPTER 29

'Naseer's still at the hotel,' said Sanjeewa. 'You have Layla and Ashok to thank for that. They realised how distressed he'd be by Dev's death and saw to it that he didn't need to leave until he was ready. Ashok has plans to find him other work with the company. If you come over here, I'll arrange for him to meet us in my office. I suggest you come in through the staff entrance to the hotel this time. People might be beginning to wonder why the hotel's receiving so many visits from the police.'

'Very well.'

'I've also checked with the restaurant manager. Mr Patel came down to dinner on his own the night before Dev died. He said something about his wife being unwell and staying in their suite.'

Naseer was waiting with Sanjeewa when de Silva arrived. The pouches under his eyes were dark with shadow. He looked as if the weight of the world had fallen on his shoulders. De Silva felt sorry for him. If he and Dev had been close since boyhood, he was facing the loss of a friend as well as an employer. He must try to reassure him that he wasn't in any trouble to add to his woes. 'Please, sit down,' he said gently.

Naseer cast a glance at Sanjeewa who nodded, and they all sat.

'I'm sorry for your loss,' de Silva went on. 'This must be a very sad time for you.'

'For everyone who cared about Dev. Ashok told me he was murdered, and you've arrested Salman.' He shook his head. 'I won't believe he did it, whatever you say.' He clenched his fists. 'If I ever catch up with the bastard who did…'

Although de Silva strongly disapproved of the public taking the law into their own hands, he didn't comment. The man was entitled to express his feelings. In the circumstances, he could also understand why Ashok had ignored the instruction to keep the fact of the murder within the family.

'We may have a lead that will enable us to find out who that person is and clear Salman's name, but to take it any further, I need your help.'

A flicker of hope passed across Naseer's face. 'I'll do anything you ask.'

'Have you spent much time in the main areas of the hotel?'

'Very little. Whilst the filming was going on, I was on the set every day. It's only since….' He took a deep breath. 'Since Dev passed away that I've stayed at the hotel all the time and then usually in my room. I take my meals in the kitchens.'

'I need to know if you recognise one of the guests. I believe Dev may have been acquainted with her, perhaps a long time ago.'

'Where will I find her?'

Sanjeewa looked at his wristwatch. 'It's gone seven o'clock. She and her husband are booked in to have dinner at eight and usually come down for a drink beforehand.' He rang the bell on his desk. 'We'd better get you into suitable clothes. One of my staff will make sure you see her, if not in the bar, then in the restaurant.'

'And I'll be waiting here for the result,' said de Silva.

'Is there always so much time spent waiting in police work?' asked Sanjeewa as the minutes ticked by.

De Silva laughed. 'An hour or so is nothing, my friend. I fear your ideas are too much influenced by detective stories in books where there has to be action on every page.'

'What will you do if Naseer recognises Mrs Patel?'

'That depends on what he has to say about her.'

'I can tell you that she and her husband are rich. Although,' he added irritably, 'from the way Mrs Patel haggles over every penny the hotel charges, you might wonder if their reputation for being so is unfounded.'

'I've heard it said that the poor are often more generous than the rich.'

'That certainly fits Mrs Patel. On the other hand, Dev Khan wasn't afraid to spend his money.' Sanjeewa frowned. 'I'm not sure how much is left for the family. Something Ashok Mehta once said made me wonder if the Khan family's finances were in as good a shape as his style of living suggested.'

'Interesting. If Mrs Patel had something to do with Dev's death, might money be involved?'

Before they had time to explore the thought, there was a knock at the door. One of the staff showed Naseer in.

'Well?' asked de Silva.

Naseer's expression was grim. 'I recognised her alright. It was a long time ago, but she's not changed much. Still the same ugly face and spiteful expression. Her name was Chaudhary then. She kept a brothel in the slum district of Bombay where Dev and I grew up. There were rumours she was behind quite a few murders where the killers were never caught.'

'Did Dev know her?'

'Yes, she took a fancy to him at one stage, but he did his best to keep out of her way.'

'What about Mr Patel?'

'Never seen him before.'

'Did Dev say anything to you about her being here?'

Naseer shook his head.

'And would anyone else in the family recognise her?'

'I doubt it very much.'

'Do you think she recognised you?'

'She showed no sign of it and it's a long time ago.' Naseer gave a sour smile. 'Unlike Dev, I was never much to look at.'

'Can you think of any reason why she'd want to harm Dev?'

'Revenge for slighting her all those years ago?' chipped in Sanjeewa.

Naseer shrugged.

'I think money must be involved,' said de Silva, thinking of the note. 'Was Dev in trouble financially?'

Naseer nodded. 'He hadn't dared tell Sunita or any of the family and he did his best to hide it, but he was running short of cash.'

'What about the film company?'

'Not as profitable as it used to be. Oh, there was no immediate danger, but something was going to have to change. Dev just didn't want to face it.'

'Is it possible that Dev hoped Mrs Patel might be persuaded to help him in return for silence about her past life?'

Naseer hesitated. 'He never said anything about that to me.'

Sanjeewa looked at de Silva. 'I expect you want to question her. I'd be grateful if you'd try to do so without causing a ruckus.'

'I'll do my best.'

* * *

'I've had to be rather economical with the truth to get us in there, but she's waiting in her suite,' said Sanjeewa. He was visibly flustered. 'I hope this is going to be justified, Shanti, or I doubt there'll be enough flowers and champagne in Nuala to pacify Mrs Patel.'

De Silva felt a shiver of disquiet. What if Naseer's memory wasn't reliable? And what if it was, but the evidence he had to support his case didn't stand up? Was he placing too much reliance on the words he'd heard Dev mutter the day he knocked down the gardener in his car? Apart from that and those hairpins, all he had was the crumpled note in Dev's room. Had he and Sanjeewa made a mistake in thinking the writing matched Mrs Patel's? It was safe to assume that she wasn't the kind of woman to buckle under questioning and confess to a crime. He would have to hope that her husband, if he knew what had gone on, was an easier target.

The Patels' suite was one of the grandest in the hotel. In its drawing room, turquoise silk curtains hung at the windows. The walls were decorated with wallpaper patterned with white chrysanthemums on the palest of turquoise backgrounds. A splendid Persian rug covered the centre of the floor; sofas and chairs upholstered in pale grey brocade were arranged around it. On one of them sat Mrs Patel, the scowl on her face indicating that she was ready for a fight. Her husband hovered by a window looking awkward and apprehensive. De Silva wondered if he found his wife's scenes embarrassing. Or was he too involved in Dev's murder? If he was, it was probably more than his life was worth to give anything away.

'The manager tells me there's been a complaint,' Mrs Patel snapped. 'I can't imagine why you need to be involved, Inspector.' Her eyes were daggers as she darted a disparaging look at Sanjeewa. 'A reputable hotel ought to protect its guests from impudence. In any case, we've decided to check out early.' Her eyes narrowed. 'I intend to scrutinise the bill thoroughly.'

All the while she'd been speaking, de Silva had studied her carefully, but he was unable to detect any sign of defensiveness under the bravado. As he'd anticipated, Mrs Patel was going to be a hard nut to crack.

'I'm involved because this is a police inquiry, ma'am.'

Mrs Patel puffed out her chest like a bullfrog in the mating season. She rounded on Sanjeewa. 'Why wasn't I told?'

Because if you had been, you would no doubt have refused to see me, thought de Silva. Aloud he replied, 'I am responsible for that, ma'am. I asked Mr Gunesekera to maintain the utmost discretion. The matter is an extremely sensitive one.'

'Then I suppose you'd better go on.'

'You may be aware that Dev Khan, who was shooting a film here in Nuala, died a few days ago. For several years he had suffered from a weak heart, and initially the medical opinion was that the cause of death was heart failure.'

'I wasn't aware he'd died,' said Mrs Patel. 'Of course I know the name. Over the years, my husband and I have seen some of his films, so we recognised him when we noticed him here, but when we no longer saw him about, we assumed that he'd checked out, didn't we?' She turned to her husband who nodded. 'I'm sorry to hear of his death,' she went on, 'but I can't imagine why, if you hope to keep it confidential, you're telling us.'

'Because it's come to light that his death was not due to natural causes. He was murdered. I believe you were acquainted with Mr Khan, and we are questioning everyone who knew him, and who was in the hotel at the time, as to their whereabouts.'

An impatient expression came over Mrs Patel's face. 'I've just told you, Inspector. My husband and I knew *of* him. That was all.'

'I beg to differ, ma'am. I have testimony that although it's many years ago, you knew him personally.'

Mrs Patel gave a snort of annoyance. 'Testimony? Outright nonsense is a more accurate description. I demand to know who this person is.'

'Naseer Ansari.'

'I've never heard of him.'

'But he remembers you,' persisted de Silva. 'You were living in the slum area of Bombay where he and Dev Khan grew up.'

Mrs Patel's face was a mask of fury. 'A slum area? I've never had anything to do with such places.'

Her husband, who hadn't spoken so far, stepped forward. 'Inspector, there must be some mistake,' he said quickly. 'My wife's family came from a small town in Maharashtra. It was only later in life that she moved to Bombay with her first husband. When he died, friends of the family helped her. We met shortly afterwards. If she tells you she doesn't know this man Naseer, it's the truth. He's mistaken her for someone else. Someone against whom he bears a grudge.'

De Silva took a deep breath. He couldn't back down now, whatever the consequences. 'Naseer Ansari is certain he hasn't made a mistake. Dev Khan took a daily dose of digitoxin for his heart condition. This was given to him by a nurse who travelled with him, Anne Collins. We believe your wife broke into Collins' room, stole some of that medicine and injected Dev with a fatal overdose of it.'

Mrs Patel threw back her head and emitted a cackle of laughter, then she stopped. With a look Medusa might have envied, her eyes bored into de Silva. 'The idea that I had anything to do with Dev Khan's death is ludicrous. I didn't know the man. What possible motive could I have for wanting to kill him?'

'He knew that in your early days in Bombay, you were involved in activities that you wouldn't want made public now. He was blackmailing you, wasn't he, Mrs Patel? We know that he was in financial trouble.'

The ice in Mrs Patel's voice sent a chill up de Silva's spine. 'This is a tissue of lies. I'll listen to no more of it. I insist you leave immediately. I've never been so insulted in my life.'

She rounded on Sanjeewa. 'And for exposing me to these insults, *you* will be hearing from my lawyers.'

'Please calm yourself, ma'am,' said de Silva. 'If as you claim, you had nothing to do with Dev Khan's death, you have nothing to fear, but for the moment you're under arrest.'

CHAPTER 30

'Have you had a good day, my love?' asked de Silva when he arrived home a few evenings later.

'It's been a quiet one,' said Jane. 'I had letters to write then I'd promised to look out some things for the next jumble sale in aid of the church, so I got on with that. I'm sure you've had a much more interesting time. Don't keep me in suspense.'

He grinned. 'Just long enough to pour myself a well-earned whisky and soda. A sherry for you?'

'That would be very nice.'

He poured their drinks, and they went out to the verandah. De Silva took a sip of his whisky then sat down. 'Well, there have been a few developments concerning the Patels. I'm fairly certain that Mrs Patel's husband didn't know what she was up to, but Archie has taken the view that he ought to be arrested as well and charged with conspiracy.'

'Do you think he'll be found innocent?'

'Hard to say. Even if he is, effectively he'll be punished. My impression of him is that he's a follower, not a leader. Sanjeewa thinks he's from a wealthy family and his money comes from them rather than his own endeavours. Sadly, it was probably the knowledge that she would be able to make him dependent on her for everything except money that attracted Mrs Patel to him. Without her, I suspect he'll be all at sea.'

'Where are they now?'

'Still in the cells at the station, but they'll be taken down to Kandy in the next day or so, then the authorities there will take over. I've already sent them the bottle that we found in Mrs Patel's toilet bag after the Patels were arrested. Hebden thinks the small amount of liquid that's in it is digitoxin. Presumably, she decanted a quantity from the bottle in Anne Collins' room but didn't use it all. She didn't need to steal a syringe. She has health problems herself and injects her own medication each day.'

'So she was accustomed to using a syringe.'

'Yes. Hebden and I thought the person who injected Dev might not be, but the clumsy execution was probably because he was struggling at the time.'

Billy trotted up the steps from the garden followed by Bella who jumped onto de Silva's lap. She pressed the side of her head against his hand and purred as he scratched her gently behind the ears.

'How do you think Mrs Patel knew about Dev's weak heart?' asked Jane, bending to stroke Billy who had come to sit at her feet. His lips stretched in a yawn, displaying needle-sharp pearly teeth in the small pink cavern of his mouth.

'She struck up a conversation with Raj and his girlfriend. I imagine she was hoping to find out something that would help her to plan her crime and she succeeded. It would be easy for a clever woman like her to get information out of them. As for how she found out where Anne Collins' room was, one of the receptionists remembers her asking if a friend of hers called Mary Collins was booked in at the hotel. The friend was fictitious, but Mrs Patel made a great fuss about it. The receptionist became flustered and turned the registration book around so she could see for herself that there was no Mary Collins. That would have given her the opportunity to take note of Anne Collins' room number.

As for how she managed to get into the room, no keys or staff overalls were reported missing, so I expect she picked the lock as we thought she might have done.'

'Do you think she planned to kill Dev from the beginning?'

'Impossible to be sure and of course she's refusing to talk. She may have been prepared to pay something but then been afraid he'd always demand more.'

'I hope Archie isn't very put out about the way all this has ended. Florence said that even though he was dubious at first, he became very enthusiastic about how hosting a film company would put Nuala on the map.'

'Nuala is on the map. Isn't the possession of a famous detective enough?'

Jane laughed and shook her head. 'You know perfectly well what I mean. A successful film that was set here might have brought more business to the town. Nuala might have become a tourist attraction. Once the war's over, I'm sure travel will become popular again. Tea growing's all very well but—'

'Best not to keep all one's eggs in one box?'

'Basket, dear.'

'There's no reason why the film won't still be a success. The rest of the Khan family seem determined to finish it. It appears that most of the scenes that involved Dev have already been filmed and ways can be found around those that haven't.'

'Who told you that?'

'Ashok. By the way, he's invited us to join him and Layla at the Crown for a drink this evening. They'll be leaving Nuala soon and they didn't want to go without saying goodbye.'

'That was a kind thought. He seems such a nice young man. I'm sure he'll do his best to make her happy.'

'I'm sure he will. And Layla will need his support. I

believe she'll be the member of the family that mourns her father the most deeply.'

'Aren't you being a little hard on his wife and stepsons?'

'I don't mean to be. People get out of life what they put into it. If the relationship between them and Dev wasn't a happy one, he had to bear some of the blame.'

'What about Nurse Collins? Is she still at the Crown?'

'I'm not sure. After I told Sanjeewa she could be released, she came to see me and said she'd be leaving Nuala, but she didn't say when.'

'How did she seem?'

'Very sad. I felt sorry for her. She talked of looking for a new job in Colombo. I suppose she's given up all hope of her relationship with Raj being rekindled.'

CHAPTER 31

Ashok was alone in the bar at the Crown when the de Silvas arrived that evening. He stood up to greet them.

'We're so glad you could come,' he said. 'Layla will be down soon. She's looking forward to seeing you. Hari and Salman also want to join us.'

Whilst they waited, they ordered drinks: whisky for Ashok and de Silva and sherry for Jane. When they arrived, Ashok raised his glass. 'To you, Inspector! If it hadn't been for you, matters would have turned out very differently. Dev will be greatly missed, but given time and everyone's agreement, we have the opportunity to take the company in a new direction.'

'You're very kind, but I mustn't take all the credit.'

Ashok smiled. 'I'm sure you're being too modest.' He lowered his voice. 'I wouldn't say this if Layla was with us, but I'm afraid Dev's ideas were becoming old-fashioned, and to add to the problem, his projects gobbled money. The company was in danger of getting into serious financial difficulties. Hari has a lot of interesting ideas, and Salman will be able to take advantage of the opportunities to write more modern scripts, as he's been keen to do for some time.'

He looked up. 'Ah, here they come now.'

Layla wore a full-skirted white dress trimmed with lace. She carried a small red-leather purse, and her high-heeled shoes were a matching shade of red. Her shiny black hair fell in soft waves to her shoulders. Hari and Salman were also smartly dressed in cream trousers and navy jackets. They greeted Jane and de Silva with smiles and shook hands.

'My stepmother sends her apologies,' Layla said in her gentle voice when they'd all sat down. 'She doesn't feel up to being in company yet.' Her eyes misted and Ashok squeezed her hand.

'It's perfectly understandable for her to want time on her own,' said Jane sympathetically. 'It must be hard for you too. We do so appreciate your spending time with us.'

Layla smiled. 'It's a pleasure. I'm very grateful to your husband.' She tucked her arm into Ashok's. 'Sunita and I plan to stay a few more days in Nuala and let the others go down to Colombo. Ashok thought he ought to stay with us, but we'll be fine on our own. And you'll have a lot to get on with in Colombo,' she added, turning to Ashok.

He smiled. 'You see, she's telling me what to do already.'

Salman was also smiling. It was the first time de Silva had seen him do so and it transformed his face. He and Hari sat next to each other on one of the bar's deep leather sofas. They appeared to be totally relaxed.

They chatted about the company's plans for a while then de Silva noticed Raj and his girlfriend come into the bar. Raj raised a hand in salute, and they walked over. Like the other men, he wore cream trousers and a smart jacket, but he'd added a peacock-blue and gold patterned silk cravat. His girlfriend was strikingly attired in an off-the-shoulder white dress. He proceeded to monopolise the conversation and de Silva was relieved when the couple took their leave. The encounter had done nothing to change de Silva's view that Raj wasn't particularly distressed by his stepfather's passing. He wondered how much the actor knew about the relationship between his brother and Hari Bedu. Perhaps the easy way they had behaved together this evening indicated that he was aware of it, and with Dev gone felt he had more freedom to accept it. The same might apply to the rest of the family. De Silva hoped that was the case.

The little party had broken up and the de Silvas were about to get into the Morris to drive home when de Silva heard a voice calling them. He turned and in the light from the hotel windows, made out Hari and Salman. They waited for them to catch up.

'We didn't want to say anything in there,' said Hari, 'but we couldn't let you go without a special thank you from us.' He hesitated. 'Even before we heard about Dev's murder, we'd decided we had to go our own ways.'

So, thought de Silva, that would explain why Salman had seemed so distressed when he'd found him at the hotel.

'I imagine I don't need to explain to you what our reasons for the decision were,' Hari went on. 'But your kindness and help has changed our minds. You gave us hope that a time will come when the world isn't against us, and that means so much.'

'I was glad to be of assistance. I wish you both good luck.'

'Thank you.'

'I'm afraid life will never be easy for them,' said Jane as Hari and Salman headed back to the hotel. 'But thanks to you, this time at least they're out of danger.'

'Let's hope it stays that way.'

CHAPTER 32

It was still dark when de Silva, Prasanna, and Nadar, seeing their way by torchlight and accompanied by Archie and a few of the Residence's outdoor staff, headed for the wood where de Silva and Nadar had found the peacock's nest on their previous visit. They had with them the large bamboo cage that Nadar had constructed. To transport it, long poles had been slid between the bars on either side, and the Residence staff used them to carry it along.

'I hope this is going to work,' muttered Archie. For once, Darcy wasn't by his side. The old Labrador had whined when he was left in the house but if he'd known the errand they were going on, thought de Silva, he would have been happy not to be included.

'Don't worry, sir, it will,' whispered Nadar. De Silva wished he felt equally confident. What would they do if the peacock was on the nest, or if it surprised them before they were ready for it? He cast a sideways glance at Prasanna who looked a little queasy, or was it the effect of the moonlight?

His immediate fears were allayed when they reached the clearing and found the nest occupied only by the peacock's treasures. They appeared to have increased in number since de Silva last saw them and now included some bottle tops from Elephant ginger beer bottles, a small tin can, and even a few strands of tinsel. De Silva couldn't imagine where that had been filched from.

With Nadar directing operations, some of the under-growth was cut down then the cage put in its place and covered with the branches so that only the entrance was visible. Using two stout sticks, Nadar jacked up the moving panel that provided a door then tied ropes to the sticks. After that he produced a box and spread the pieces of fig inside it from the threshold all the way to the back of the cage. He stood back and surveyed his work. 'That should do it.' He dusted off his hands. 'Prasanna and I'll stay close, but I suggest everyone else waits further away.'

De Silva and the others took up their positions behind the trees that Nadar had indicated. No one spoke as the first glimmer of light penetrated the tree canopy and the wood began to come alive with birds singing and flitting from branch to branch. There were scuffling and crackling sounds. De Silva wondered what small animals made them. Close to him, a piece of bark on the trunk of a tree that had fallen at a slant seemed to move. He stiffened, fearful it was a snake, but then realised it was a frog, its scaly, greenish-brown body a perfect camouflage. It flicked out its long tongue to catch an insect, and its yellow eyes bulged, giving it a sinister air. The image of Mrs Patel rose in de Silva's mind. He wondered how the Kandy police were progressing with the case. It was a relief that it wasn't his responsibility any longer.

Suddenly, a harsh, eerie cry cut through the mellifluous noises of the wood. Was the peacock on its way back to its nest? A few moments passed then there was a flash of green and blue as it appeared, flying low in the clumsy style that always seemed to him to be so out of keeping with a peacock's elegant, spectacular plumage. It landed heavily, folded its wings, and proceeded to peck at the floor of the clearing, at first ignoring the cage. De Silva's heart sank. But after a while, its head jerked up and it noticed the food Nadar had put down. It ambled over and began to eat, slowly moving further into the cage until its whole body was inside. Nadar and Prasanna, who had been waiting in the bushes holding the ropes, pulled the sticks away and the door clattered down. A cheer rose from the onlookers.

CHAPTER 33

The vicarage garden looked beautiful in the morning sunshine with old-fashioned roses that gave off a honeyed scent, beds of pink and white geraniums, and luxuriant displays of more exotic plants that were native to Ceylon.

'The minute Jane told me about your peacock,' said Mrs Peters, 'I knew that my prayers had been answered.' The vicar's wife had a beaming smile on her homely face. 'The peahen who adopted us recently has been so lonely. I fear her mate was killed by poachers. Now she can have a companion again.'

The bamboo cage had been deposited on the vicarage lawn an hour previously. At first when the door panel was lifted, the peacock had been reluctant to emerge but eventually his confidence returned. He and the peahen were now foraging side by side for insects in the grass.

And showing the placidly contented air of an elderly couple who no longer need to voice every thought to communicate with one another, thought de Silva with amusement.

'Now that he's settled in, I insist you stay for breakfast to celebrate,' Mrs Peters continued.

'How kind,' said Florence. Prasanna, Nadar, and the Residence's outdoor staff had gone home after the peacock had been delivered to the vicarage, but she and Jane had joined Archie and de Silva.

The four of them and Reverend and Mrs Peters took their places at the table that had been laid on the terrace. De Silva hadn't been sure what to expect but he was soon thoroughly enjoying the meal of creamy scrambled eggs, fresh fruit, hot-buttered muffins, and homemade strawberry jam, washed down by strong tea poured from a large brown-earthenware teapot.

'How clever of you to catch the peacock, Inspector,' remarked Mrs Peters.

'The credit is really due to my young officers, ma'am.' He had decided that even though Nadar deserved the lion's share, he didn't want to leave Prasanna out. He had pulled away one of the sticks, and getting close enough to do that had presumably required him to overcome some of his fear of the bird.

'It's good of you to give them the credit,' said Mrs Peters with a smile. She picked up the teapot. 'Another cup? And could you manage one more muffin?'

De Silva patted his stomach. 'It was all delicious, ma'am, but I think I must stop there.'

Breakfast over, he, Archie, and Reverend Peters left the ladies to talk and went to inspect the vicar's new fishpond. He had explained at breakfast that the old one was becoming far too small for his collection of koi carp.

The new pond sparkled in the sunshine. Pads of water lilies with showy pink and white flowers dotted the surface and the jewel-coloured koi darted between them like giant fireflies.

'Fine collection you have, vicar,' remarked Archie. 'Not much eating on them though.'

The vicar chuckled. 'No, purely decorative, I'm afraid. But like our new peacock, they remind one of how glorious God's creation is.'

'Indeed.'

The vicar peered over the top of his spectacles in the

direction of the terrace. 'My wife is summoning me. Would you excuse me, gentlemen?'

'Of course. Mustn't keep ladies waiting,' said Archie jocularly.

'Decent chap, Peters,' he remarked as the vicar hurried off towards the terrace. 'Even if he'll never make a fisherman. Shall we walk a bit further?'

'With pleasure.'

They walked in silence for a couple of minutes before Archie spoke.

'Grateful to you for solving the peacock trouble, and of course poor Dev Khan's murder. I visited the family before they left Nuala to offer my condolences again. They seem to be coping. I've heard from Kandy that the Patels' case comes to trial in a few weeks. William Petrie believes she'll be convicted but Patel has a chance of getting off.'

'I think that would be the right result.'

'Going back to the peacock,' Archie went on. 'It's a great relief to have things back on an even keel at the Residence.' He grinned. 'Mrs Clutterbuck has stopped bending my ear, and poor old Darcy has a spring in his step for his walks again. Your constable did an excellent job. Mustn't forget your sergeant as well. I expect he played a part. I've thought more about that pay rise you asked me about and decided a good job done merits a reward. I'll leave it with you to thrash out the details. Within reason, you can be confident that whatever you recommend will be signed off.'

'Thank you, sir. I'm sure they'll be very grateful.'

'Good. I'm glad that's settled. Shall we rejoin the party?'

As they walked to the terrace, Archie went back to talking about fishing. Only half listening, de Silva thought of the peacock. It was funny how something as small as a rogue bird had the power to bring about change. If it hadn't been for the peacock, Prasanna and Nadar might have waited a long time. Perhaps after all was said and done, the way to make the world a better place was for each person to look for the small things they could do and hope that eventually, they would amount to one big thing. He smiled to himself. He was looking forward to giving Prasanna and Nadar the good news.

* * *

'Goodness, what an eventful time it's been,' said Jane as they drove home from the vicarage. The sun was getting high in the sky and the heat was rapidly increasing. De Silva was glad of the breeze that was stirred up as they went along.

'Truth really has been stranger than fiction,' continued Jane. 'Dev Khan must hardly have believed his luck when he saw Mrs Patel coming into the Crown. I imagine he thought his money troubles were over, but of course as it turned out he was far from lucky.'

'Yes, clearly Mrs Patel isn't a woman to cross.'

'I must say,' Jane went on, 'the cook at the vicarage puts on a wonderful spread.'

De Silva nodded, thinking of hot-buttered muffins slathered with strawberry jam.

'We'll hardly need lunch.' She turned her head to look at him. 'Don't look so glum.'

'I wasn't,' he said, not entirely truthfully.

They drove on in silence for a while.

'Isn't it wonderful that the peacock and the Peters' peahen took to each other so quickly,' remarked Jane. 'Mrs Peters says they're going to call them Fred and Ginger. I was wondering—' There was another silence.

'Wondering what?' asked de Silva when it became too pregnant to ignore.

'Well, peacocks are so beautiful, aren't they? What fun it would be to have one ourselves.'

De Silva felt a stirring of alarm as he thought about the damage a peacock might do to his garden, to say nothing of the danger of being imprisoned in the bungalow if it decided not to let him out. 'No,' he said with all the firmness he could muster. 'I don't think that would be a good idea at all.'

'Whyever not?'

'For one thing, Billy and Bella wouldn't allow it.'

Jane chuckled. 'I wish you could see your face, Shanti. Of course I was only joking.'

His shoulders went down. 'That's a relief.' He slowed the Morris and they turned into Sunnybank's drive.

'Oh, I forgot to mention,' said Jane as the car came to a halt outside the bungalow. 'This week's film at the cinema looks fun. It's a comedy with George Formby. Shall we go this evening? That is if you haven't had enough of the film world to last you for a very long time.'

De Silva turned off the engine, applied the handbrake then got out and came around to her side of the car to open the door. 'If you want to see it, I'm happy to go. Just as long as all I need to do is watch.'

Jane smiled. 'I think I can promise you that.'

She stood up and slipped an arm through his. 'But I'm sure that if you start to miss the excitement, another adventure will soon come along.'

* * *

215